The Girl from Tir-na-nOg

Gary Hope

"The Girl From Tir-na-nOg," by Gary Hope. ISBN 978-1-62137-939-3 (softcover); 978-1-62137-940-9 (eBook).

Published 2016 by Virtualbookworm.com Publishing Inc., P.O. Box 9949, College Station, TX , 77842, US.

No matter how chaotic it is, wildflowers will still spring up in the middle of nowhere.

Table of Contents

1

THE JUDGE LOOKED at me and asked, "Do you have any questions, Mr. Alfred?"

I tried to look as heartbroken as possible as I answered, "No, your Honor, I understand completely." He banged his gavel and walked out of the courtroom.

My lawyer shook my hand and said, "I'm sorry Paul, not a very good birthday present for you." And so, the first day of my 31st year began. My now ex-wife and her lawyer (who is soon to be her new husband) hugged and kissed and laughed.

I hung my head and slowly shuffled out of the courtroom as I began to celebrate my 31st birthday the way I'd been planning it for a year now. You see, one year ago is when my wife (now ex-wife) informed me she had become pregnant, had an abortion and wanted a divorce. Two of those three events took me by great surprise. Since I hadn't had sexual relations with her in over two years, I was pretty sure I wasn't the father. That she'd had an abortion also surprised me, since I had no idea she was even pregnant.

It did not surprise me she wanted a divorce. That, in fact, was a relief. We were never really suited or compatible with each other, except that I liked a pretty face and long legs, which she had. And she liked a lot of money, which she THOUGHT I had. We both became quickly disappointed. Once she figured out that I wasn't the rich guy she thought I was, her entire personality changed.

She thought by marrying me she would have unlimited credit cards, new cars, a nice big house, and unlimited vacations all over the world. It took about eighteen months before reality truly sunk in and she realized the fairy tale life she dreamed of had evaporated.

I'm a building contractor here in Winston-Salem, mainly building houses and a few small office buildings. I built the house where we live; though on paper, it is actually owned by my company, not me personally. She never figured that out. Also, my truck and the cars we both drove are owned by the company. When the economy was booming, our business boomed. People wanted new houses and everything seemed rosy. Conversely, when the economy slowed, our business slowed and my wife became unhappy—very unhappy. I have four large houses under construction and one small office building nearly completed, all of which are financed through banks with liens and mortgages out the wazoo.

If I could hang on and eventually sell the houses and office building, everything would be grand and all the debts would be paid off. That was a big "If." The economy turned south; the buyers backed out and I was left with unfinished properties and huge debts. On paper, I still looked good. Gina (my now ex-wife) thought I looked good; everyone thought I looked good. I probably could have endured this downturn and re-financed this and that and eventually come out ahead. That was one year ago. Things changed.

I knew our marriage wasn't working out. We were both unhappy but I was hoping that when the economy picked up, our fortunes would change. I was dreaming. I came home from work one day to find Gina and her lawyer, Charles, waiting for me in the living room. At the time I didn't know Charles, but I knew his kind. In every profession there's good people and bad people. You'll find good truck drivers and careless ones, good baseball players and minor leaguers, good guitar players and hacks, good lawyers and snakes like Charles.

This was the night I found out about Gina's pregnancy and abortion. Charles informed me that the abortion had been completed at a local clinic run by his brother, and he preceded to show me the documentation when I told them I didn't believe it. It wasn't that I didn't believe Gina had an abortion—with Gina, anything was possible. What I didn't believe was that I was the father, unless her pregnancy had lasted over two years.

Since the abortion clinic didn't take any DNA samples from the fetus to prove who the father could have been, it was now Gina's word against mine. Charles also informed me they would be filing for divorce and suing for half of my company, half of our total assets, the entire house and a huge financial payment for Gina's emotional and physical abuse from me "forcing" her to get the abortion. Wow, Charles was good.

As I started processing all this information, I also started looking at my options. There weren't many. I talked to several friends and learned some valuable information along the way. Apparently, Charles and some of his "posse" had been spreading rumors and innuendos about me and my solvency throughout the business community in our town. He also convinced or coerced all the customers I had for the houses and commercial property that I would soon be declaring bankruptcy. He suggested they should all bail out before it was too late.

Fortunately for me, I had total confidence in Charles's ability to make me look like the worst husband and worst businessman in history. Forcing his wife to have an abortion—how cruel can I be? That night is when I started planning my escape. Each week I began taking a little money out of the checking accounts, both the personal and the company accounts. Not enough to raise any eyebrows, but enough. I started paying the minimum (or less) on all the bills owed by the company and our personal credit cards. Then I asked all the creditors to lend me some time. Since I'd been a long-term customer, they all accommodated me.

I continued to empty all the accounts and kept all the proceeds in cash, well hidden. I was also able to secure second and third mortgages on my house and properties. I also got what personal loans I could get from banks and credit unions, based on my past histories with them, using our house as collateral. All of these loans were also converted to cash over a period of time. It wasn't a lot, but it would be enough to get me away and settled until I could find employment. In the meantime, my lovely wife had maxed out all her credit cards, which she and her lawyer/lover thought I was paying off. I also discovered they had been carrying on their secret affair for almost two years while skimming money from my savings accounts in the process. And they were now living together in MY house, completely unaware of what was just about to happen to them.

I was preparing to not only give Gina half of everything, I was going to give her the whole enchilada. All the bills, all the debt, all the liens and all the trouble! I was sure she and Charles could figure it all out when I was gone. Where was I going? I was going somewhere I'd never heard of. Somewhere I'd never be found, someplace where I could disappear and live happily ever after. I was going to Dungloe, County Donegal, Republic of Ireland.

I walked out of the courtroom that day, got in my car, which was on the verge of being repossessed, and drove to Norfolk, Virginia. I had a suitcase packed with essential clothing and another smaller bag stuffed with cash. I'd been going to Norfolk for several weeks in the hopes of meeting someone I could bribe. It didn't take long. I was looking for someone who worked in the freighter business. There were several bars in the dock area and it wasn't hard making acquaintances, especially when you floated around hundred dollar bills.

I met a guy about my age, with similar features who volunteered to let me use his visa for the next voyage back on a working freighter to Hamburg, Germany. When I say "volunteered" I mean bribed. A couple of thousand dollars is a lot of money to a drunk in a bar. I promised to mail him the visa back to Norfolk when I arrived in Hamburg. We both knew that was a lie. These freighters don't check things very closely. They just want someone to work on the ship for low wages and not ask any questions. The same thing I was looking for.

I board the ship with no problems. They simply scan over my "visa," and I start my job as a cook's helper and cleaner as I wait for the ship to leave port in two days. I was pretty sure my car wouldn't be found any time soon, since I threw the license plate away and stole one from another car in the port parking lot to replace it. Just before boarding the ship I went to the sleaziest used car lot I could find and sold the car for considerably less than it was worth. But, I didn't care; I just wanted a little extra cash. If I can make it these two days until the ship sails for Hamburg, I'll be free and clear. I did.

Aside from getting sea sick and hit on by a young ship mate, the ocean crossing was uneventful. I bought a Rail Pass in Hamburg and took the train to France, then through the Chunnel to England and up to Liverpool where I hopped a ferry over to Belfast. I'd researched

Ireland beforehand. I want a country that speaks English and has very rural, out-of-the way settings, thus the northern reaches of Ireland. I want to be away from the tourist spots in the south and west. I want to be beyond the reaches of anyone. In fact, I want to go to the back of beyond.

Dungloe was nowhere anyone wanted to go—except me.

2

GINA AND I had no children and I was an only child, except for an older brother whom I don't claim because he's a cheat, a liar, and a bum. Our parents died several years ago in a car accident and he tried his best to cheat me out of our inheritance. He nearly succeeded. There are a few remote uncles and aunts whom I haven't spoken with in years and maybe a few so-called friends. But honestly, no one will miss me except Gina and Charles. And they won't actually miss me. They'll only miss me paying their bills for them.

I'm sure old Charles will have all the authorities trying to track me down. They'll check all over the state and my hometown and maybe even a few bordering states. Gina will tell them, truthfully, that I never had a passport. And, I never did. I never travelled outside the U.S. before, except one ill-advised trip to Tijuana and once to look at the Canadian side of Niagara Falls. That's why I'm pretty sure that as long as I lay low and don't cause any problems here in Ireland, Gina and her lover boy will never find me. Of course, I'll have to change my name and have some half-way believable reason why I'm here in Dungloe. That should be easy enough, right?

My birthday was July 14. It took me a few weeks to make the ocean crossing and get to Dungloe. I wrongly assumed it would be summer in the far reaches of Ireland. It was not. When I exit the comforts of the train at the Dungloe station, the wind is blowing about 25 mph. It's also raining and feels like 40 degrees outside. Actually, I have no idea how cold it really is because all the temperatures are in Celsius. I should have paid better attention in science class my freshman year in high school.

Dungloe is situated on the west coast, in the northern part of Ireland. Aside from being cold, damp and windy, I know very little of my new home. Ever since I landed in Hamburg, I've been thinking of various stories I can tell people when they ask why I'm in Dungloe. The one that makes the most sense, and probably the easiest to explain is this:

I was born and raised in Toronto, Canada where I was a supervisor in a company that made GPS systems for cars. I was promoted and transferred to the sister plant in Birmingham, England where I trained for about six months before being permanently transferred to Belfast, Northern Ireland. My story is that I'd been working in Belfast about three years when the owners closed the factory.

I liked Ireland so I decided to stay and look for other work. I'd saved a bit of money and could afford to take my time and figure things out. While I was out exploring the region, I met a girl one night in a pub in the coastal town of Ballycastle. She was gorgeous—flaming red hair, a body to die for and for some reason, she took a liking to me. At the time it never struck me as odd that a beautiful twenty-three year old woman would start flirting with an average looking man 8 years older than her. I would soon find out the reason why.

We spent the night together in a local hotel and the next morning she asked me if I would drive her over to Donegal so she could pick up some things from her parent's house. For the promise of another night with this beauty, I'd have driven her to London and back. When we got to the border crossing from Northern Ireland into the Republic of Ireland is when things went crazy.

Usually, these border crossings are mere formalities and they just wave you on through without stopping—not this time. The guards told me to pull over onto a side road, where they then started searching me and my car and my suitcases. My so-called girlfriend jumped out of the car and disappeared somewhere. The two guards started pushing me around, asking me if I had sexually assaulted the girl and making all kinds of accusations.

At that point, a young looking girl, about 15 years old, appeared from nowhere and the guards asked her if I was the one who assaulted and kidnapped her from Ballycastle. As you can probably tell, the whole thing was a set-up to rob me, threaten me, and scare me. It did. They took my papers, my visa, most of my money, my driver's license and told me to never come back to Northern Ireland again or I would be arrested—OR WORSE!

This was going to be my story. It could explain why I spoke with no English or Irish accent and why I have no visa or driver's license or any proof of anything. Those darn British rogues robbed me of everything! I'm hoping the good people of Dungloe will believe my story.

I arrive in my new home late in the afternoon, with two suitcases and nowhere to stay. Fortunately for me, the train station is only a couple of blocks from the city center, which is where I head. Almost immediately I see a sign for The Bridge Inn on Main Street. I don't see a "bridge" in any direction, but it looks like a nice place, so I go in and asked for a room. An elderly lady asks me how long I'll be staying and I tell her I'm not sure. She doesn't seem to understand my answer, so I try explaining to her that I am moving here and looking for a home.

She says, "Well you can't live here deary; we're just an Inn."

"I know that ma'am. This is only temporary while I look for a place."

Then she smiles and says, "Me husband and I have a small apartment to let over our place that's available, if you want to see it."

"Great," I tell her, "I'd love to see it in the morning if that would be okay?"

So far, so good. There is a pub just down the block called "The Bayview Bar," which I intend on visiting as soon as I check in my room. I know we are near the ocean, but I don't see a bay of any kind, anywhere in view. However, I know most Irish pubs offer meals as well as drinks, and I am hungry. I walk in the bar and all eleven people there set their drinks down and stare at me. It isn't often a total stranger happens to walk in their midst. I nod to all and make my way to an empty table near the bar.

A middle-aged man, whom I assume works in the pub, comes to my table and says, "Plain?"

Having no idea what he means, I reply, "Excuse me?"

I think he then says, "Do you want a pint of Guinness, or something else?"

"Oh, yes, a pint of Guinness would be very nice . . . thanks."

He goes to the bar and draws the black, foaming brew and brings it back to me asking, "You from Norn Iron?"

At this point, I can try to bluff with my answers, try telling him my story, asking him to repeat himself, or just say "No." Which is what I did. I was pretty sure I wasn't from Norn Iron, wherever that is. He just shrugs his shoulders and I think he says, "Okay, let me know if you need anything else."

I had completely forgotten to order any food. After I'd drunk about half of the Guinness, I go to the bar and ask a young girl if I can order something to eat. She smiles at me and says, "Of course you can darling. That's what we do here. What would you like?" I still haven't seen a menu, so I tell her whatever she chooses will be fine with me. She cocks her head and says something that sounds like "Go bother gibb sheek." I return to my table and sit down while everyone else in the pub continues to stare at me.

After a few minutes, the young lady brings me a plate of potatoes, beans and some kind of meat. I have no idea what it is, but it tastes pretty good. I order another Guinness for dessert and drink it as the other patrons point at me and whisper. They are obviously trying to figure out who the stranger is in their little town. As I am eating I notice some movement from most of the others in the bar. Soon, two men produce guitars and a woman brings out a violin. A young kid then reaches in his coat and takes out what looks like a flute. Then they all drag their chairs over to a heavy set man who has something that resembles a large tambourine.

They never once speak a word amongst themselves, or tune their instruments. They just start playing—I mean REALLY playing. One jig after another. Occasionally the large man will sing along, but I can never understand a word he is singing. This goes on while I'm eating and finishing my second and third Guinness—my limit. I eventually finish the black brews, pay my bill and walk back to my room while the music plays on. As a light mist is falling, I think to myself, "Well, I made it through the first day of the rest of my life. It feels good."

3

I SLEPT WELL and woke later than I usually do. I'm normally an early riser, but the overcast skies and light rain falling against the window, plus the cool temperatures acted like a sedative for me. I showered, dressed and went downstairs to find the bar/pub already open and serving breakfast. I sat in a corner by myself while everyone else in the pub stared at me. This new morning crowd found it equally curious to find a stranger in their midst.

The young lady who waited on me asked me something, of which I understood about three words. I nodded and she turned and left. I hope I ordered something to eat. I looked around to find all eyes still on me, not ashamed in the least to stare directly at me as long as I held their gaze. Unfortunately for me, none of their appearances warranted a lasting glance. Most of the dozen or so patrons were either old, scraggly men who hadn't shaved in a week, or middle-aged dowagers who needed to lose more than a few pounds. So far, Ireland hasn't impressed me by its beauty.

The waitress returned to my table and set a plate in front of me that included bacon, ham, sausage, eggs, half of a tomato and baked beans. I'd never had baked beans for breakfast before, but I'm assuming it aids with the digestion of the half a pig I've been served. She also brought hot tea to drink. I'd rather have had coffee, but it seems as though I have no choice with this meal. Tea it is. I ate it all (except the tomato) and was surprised at how tasty it was, even the baked beans and the tea. The Irish obviously don't give a hoot about cholesterol or salt intake; and, since I'm now Irish by default—neither do I.

After breakfast I strolled around town exploring my new home. Not much to see, except for all the locals staring at me. It seems as though Dungloe may be the only town in Ireland in which tourists are not visiting, and who can blame them? It's out of the way, no mountains or lakes or anything "Irish" to see. Except for the pub, there's nothing really to do in Dungloe except drink and listen to music. I walked the entire downtown area in less than ten minutes and ended up back at the pub. I was beginning to get less stares now on my second day, but I was still very much an oddity.

I met with my landlady, Mrs. O'Leary, and rented a small loft from her for one year, which was the least amount of time she would commit to. It really didn't matter since we didn't sign any papers; she just took me at my word that I'd pay her on time and not damage anything. She did tell me it would be okay if I wanted to entertain any young ladies, but she frowned upon any "overnight" stays. From what I've seen in my two days around Dungloe, there are not any young ladies, or middle-aged ladies or ladies of any type that anyone would be interested in entertaining without the aid of several large glasses of Guinness.

My plan all along was to find an out-of-the-way place like Dungloe, get a meaningless job to help with expenses and live for several years as quietly and anonymously as possible. Back at the bar I started talking to the one bartender with whom I could understand the most. I asked him where I should go to find employment in Dungloe. I didn't understand the first part of his response, but he pointed to a middle-aged man sitting by himself in a corner of the bar and motioned for me to go talk to him.

This is where I met the smartest man in the world.

I'd seen this man in the bar every time I'd been in but had not really "noticed" him. He had no distinguishing features and seemed like all the other professional drinkers that were usually hanging around. The one exception was I had noticed that he had never stared at me like the rest of the people in the bar. In fact, he seemed to purposely ignore me. I also noticed that he was always alone and that none of the regulars ever spoke to him, not even to say hello, or good morning, or whatever it is that Irish people say to each other.

All of this ran through my mind as I approached his corner table. Even when I was standing across the table from him, he never acknowledged my presence until I spoke, saying, "Excuse me sir, can I ask you something?" He looked up at me and I instantly felt like a little kid who had just been caught doing something he shouldn't have been doing. He still didn't speak but I felt like I "had" to say something, as though I were guilty of some crime. So I continued, "I'm looking for work and was told you would be the man to speak with about a job."

He continued to look up at me without uttering a single word. I held his stare as long as I dared, then started shuffling from one foot to the other. At this point, I didn't know what to do. Keep standing there like a fool? Mumble some other nonsense? Demand an answer from him? Or, wait him out? Unfortunately for me, I chose to mumble some other nonsense. I said, "I notice you sort of keep to yourself a lot; if I'm bothering you, I can leave."

He then spoke the first of his many intelligent words to me, "I'm thinking. Therefore, I don't have much in common with a lot of people in here."

How was I supposed to respond to that? Agree with him? Disagree with him? Argue with him? I had no idea, so for once I chose the intelligent way and just kept my mouth shut. He kept staring at me and I kept fidgeting. I couldn't hold his stare, I didn't know what else to say. I couldn't even tell how old he was, he could've been 42 or 52; I truly had no clue. Finally, he said, "Have a seat." When I pulled the chair out to sit down, I noticed everyone else in the bar stopped what they were doing and gawked at us. I'm certain they were shocked that I was actually going to sit down with "the man" himself.

When I sat down, I told him my new name that I'd made up, Mark McCarty (which I was still getting used to) and reached across the table to shake his hand, but he didn't move. He finally said what sounded like, "My name's Allen." But it didn't exactly sound like "Allen." It had a funny tilt to it. I think he was perceptive enough to understand my ignorance of anything Irish, so he said, "It's spelled, A I L I N. Do the best you can. You could never pronounce my last name or spell it, so we'll just stick with Ailin for now."

He kept his stare directly at me, or through me it felt like. Then he said, "Why do you want a job Mark? Especially one here in Dungloe?"

I said, "I think it's a nice place and I'd like to settle here for a while and need a job to help with all the expenses."

He continued his stare for a few seconds and finally said, "Mark, and I doubt that's your real name, if you're going to lie to me, you can get up and walk away now. I don't do business with liars. I have a nasty habit of lying to myself all the time. But I seldom believe me, there's certainly no reason I'm going to believe you."

Dang! Busted already. What do I do? We continued our stares, although he was much better than me. I had nowhere to go and nothing to lose, but I couldn't tell him the whole truth, so I compromised. I told him part of the truth, but not all of it. I told him I needed a fresh start, away from a woman, and that I was not in any trouble with the law and was not a fugitive. I shared that I had a college degree and experience running a business, managing and supervisors others. I simply wanted a place to begin again.

It took him a few moments to process this, while I waited cracking my knuckles beneath the table and trying not to break out in a cold sweat. He finally said, "Can I trust you?"

"Absolutely." I replied, and I meant it.

"Can you start work in the morning?'

"Yes, I can."

And with that, he got up, looked at me again and said, "Meet me here at half eight." He turned and walked up the stairs behind the bar as I sat trying to understand what the devil "half eight" was.

4

I was at the bar at 7:30 the next morning—unsure if "half eight" meant 7:30 or 8:30, but I didn't want to be late on my first day. It actually meant 8:30 as I found when Ailin came down the steps at 8:29. We walked outside and he pointed up the street then down the street and said, "I own most of what you see. It's not much, but I'm proud of it and proud of my town and country. Everything you see here was closed down and out of business before I bought it and began opening up various businesses. I believe in my people and I believe in Ireland. I don't know where you're from, Mark, but I know you're not Irish. However, as long as you work for me, you are Irish! Do you understand that?"

"Yes sir, I do."

He then looked at me and said, "When I was younger, I thought that money was the most important thing in life; now that I'm older, I know that it's really only second, behind love. I can't control love, but I do need someone to help me control these financial and business matters. I need an assistant to do things for me, someone who can think on their own and who doesn't need to be told everything. I know, in no uncertain terms, Mark, that there is no one like that in this town. No one that I would trust anyway. Most of the people are simple and uneducated. The young ones only care about getting drunk and the old ones stay drunk. But they're my friends and family; I love them all. I don't know what's in your past that you're hiding from, that's none of my business. But I do know that it's never too late to be what you might've been. So, are you looking for a challenge, Mark?"

I might as well start being honest with him, "My name's not actually Mark, but I sort of like the sound of it now, so yes, I'm ready."

We didn't discuss hours, salary or job descriptions. He was trusting me, so now, I'm trusting him. We toured all the businesses Ailin owned and he introduced me all around and instructed his employees, in no uncertain terms, that MY word was HIS word. I could tell right away, no one crossed Ailin. We met back at the bar over drinks and he further explained things to me. I wouldn't be handling any money or be involved in financial matters. He didn't trust me that much. But I would be his liaison and lieutenant to relieve him of the petty details of running so many enterprises.

He told me not to get my feelings hurt if he needed me to be the bartender one day, or the cashier at a restaurant he owned the next day, or the delivery man for a feed store the following day. He only needed someone he could trust. We still never discussed salary. However, he did inform me that my bar and restaurant meals were taken care of, as well as my rent. They would all be a part of my salary. Great, but still no mention of actual money. I didn't want to push the issue or jeopardize a good thing so I didn't bring it up either.

I still wasn't accustomed to the weather in my new home. It had rained every day and the temperature never reached 60 degrees. But since I still couldn't read a Celsius thermometer, I didn't actually know what it was, other than not warm. I listened to live music every night in the pub and loved it. They never seemed to play the same song twice. I watched the crowd and they watched me. I only wish there were some of them worth watching more closely.

Ailin had me doing menial tasks the first several days. I generally hung around the bar and helped out. I'd look over invoices and paperwork, order supplies, and help stock the storerooms. It was basically anything that needed doing. We'd usually spend an hour or so each evening sitting around the table, drinking a Guinness or two discussing anything and everything— but usually not work. He gave me some sound advice at the end of my first week, "Learn not to say too much." Then, he said, "Correct me if I'm wrong, but I don't think you'll be wanting taxes taken out of your salary, will you Mark?" Before I could affirm that, since I had no legitimate identity to begin with, he handed me an envelope with 750 Euros in it. Since all my meals and my rent were taken care of, I was hoping for a couple of hundred Euros at best. Before I could say anything, he got up and said,

"See you Monday," and walked up the stairs behind the bar.

So ended my first week in my new home, with my new identity, in my new life. Pretty darned good. Now if it would just stop raining!

I got my wish. I woke up Saturday morning to brilliant sunshine and fairly warm temps. Well, warm for Ireland. It's true what I'd heard about 37 shades of green. With the sun shining, everything looked different. Flowers suddenly bloomed, fields exploded in mesmerizing shades of green. Trees fulfilled their potential and everyone smiled. It was a different country—intoxicating, breathtaking, exhilarating, stimulating, and enchanting.

I went to the local restaurant, owned by Ailin, for breakfast and had another meat-laced meal. However, I got coffee this time. A plain-looking woman about my age served me and she was very friendly. I could understand almost everything she said. She had her red hair tied up in a bun, wore an ankle length dress, wore no makeup, yet, seemed attractive in an Amish sort of way.

Upon refilling my coffee for the second time, she asked me if I was the American now working for Ailin, the one they were supposed to listen to. I said that I did indeed work for Ailin, but she should choose for herself who she listened or didn't listen to. And keeping to my story, I lied, saying that I was Canadian, not American. She then replied, "If I, or anyone else around here, wants to keep their job, as I do, then all of us will indeed listen to whatever Ailin says. And now you as well."

I asked what her name was and she said, "Claire Fitzgerald, and you and I both know you're not Canadian. You don't have that accent and you're a bit too full of yourself. You're American alright." She stood there, coffee pot in hand, staring down at me waiting for an answer. Since I didn't know whether to lie, or tell her to mind her own business, or eat some bacon, I just stared back and said nothing. She finally walked away and I must admit, I was a bit relieved.

I was glad I didn't have to wait for her to bring me a bill for the food, since all my meals were taken care of by Ailin. All I had to do was leave her a tip for the service and walk out. I wondered if Ailin had, in fact, figured out I was an American and had said something to her. Or perhaps she made a lucky guess waiting for me to confirm what she thought. At any rate, I decided I'd stay away from the restaurant for a few days and definitely stay away from Claire Fitzgerald and her nosy, Amish questions.

I found myself quite alone Sunday morning, except for the rain which had returned. It seems as though everyone in town is at church, being the good Catholics they all are. All except Ailin and three other cars I saw parked at the small Baptist church at the end of town. This would make sense since Ireland was about 95% Catholic, but it did surprise me that Ailin was at the Baptist church. I assumed him to be 100% Irish in everything including religion.

5

MONDAY MORNING I decided to have a talk with Ailin. Although I didn't feel I could be completely honest with him about my situation yet, I did feel I needed to be more honest with him than I'd been so far. If Claire Fitzgerald could see through me as easily as she did, certainly someone like Ailin could as well.

We sat in our usual corner table at the pub, he had tea and I had coffee. I told him I wanted to clear the air a bit between us. He just nodded and sipped his tea. I re-emphasized that I was in no legal trouble at all (that I was aware of). I was not a fugitive and was not dangerous. I did, in fact, have a college degree and had run a business for many years. He just nodded and sipped his tea.

I then told him I was indeed an American, but I didn't see where that made any difference. At this point, he stopped me and set his cup of tea down. He said, "I don't like being lied to Mark; that's basically why I've asked you no questions. I didn't want you to lie to me. A man shouldn't have to be ashamed of where he's from. He shouldn't have to be ashamed of his country and deny it. Whatever reason you have, you're safe with me. However, I somewhat understand how you feel about America, especially these days."

I didn't know what he meant by that, but my nationalistic pride was hurt a bit, so I asked him what he was referring to. I should've left well enough alone. He said, "Mark, everyone in the world, whether they admit it or not, admires America—EVERYONE! However, in the last several years America has been changing. Not from events outside, but from powers within. Powers that are changing your country." I was a little hurt, a little mad, and a lot confused.

"What happened to the land of the free and home of the brave? America used to stand up for what was right. You sacrificed, you cared about your neighbors. You were a beacon of hope and an example of good to the world— America used to reach for the stars. America had backbone. America didn't scare so easily, Mark. The world needs America to stand up to these terrorist pricks and let them know you're not going to take it anymore. America needs to be what the rest of the world can't!

Mark, America can be all those things again. America has to be the role model for the rest of the world. It has to lead. America has to set an example for the rest of us! Whatever has happened in your past, my friend, don't ever be ashamed of your great country. Be proud!"

I wasn't sure if I wanted to punch Ailin in the nose, or shake his hand. Before I could decide, he said, "I've got to run over to Donegal this morning, make sure things are okay here. And, by the way, I hear you might be asking Claire Fitzgerald out on a date."

"WHAT?" But he was already walking away towards the door. Asking Claire out on a date? Where in the world did that come from? If I did want to date someone, it certainly wouldn't be with the town's resident plain-Jane Amish girl.

What I needed to do right now was to find a safe place to store the cash I had brought with me. I don't have a lot left after the bribe I paid and the expenses I've had. But I don't want to lose it either. I have it hidden in a bag of dirty clothes in my room now. I felt it would be safe there, but I want a more secure place . . . just in case. I can't take it to the local bank because Ailin is Chairman of the Board and would know if I deposited anything. So, after checking with all the businesses to make sure everything was fine, I take the local bus over to the closest town, Burtonport.

Even though Burtonport couldn't have been more than 10 miles away from Dungloe, in reality, it was a lifetime away. People in Ireland, especially in the north, tended to be born, raised, live and die in the same village or town. The thought of moving or visiting anywhere was completely foreign to them. In real terms, Burtonport was just as far away as Paris or London. There is a very small bank there and I rented a safe deposit box. I did not open an account because I'm sure they'd want some form of identification for that. I pay for six months in advance for the box and leave them wondering who the foreigner with the funny accent is.

I decide to have lunch in the local pub before I take the 10 mile bus ride back home. I find the only pub near the center of the little village and settle in at a table by the window. A young man comes to my table and seems overly exuberant to see me come in. I guess business is slow this morning. He asks my name, where I'm from, what sort of accent I have, what my favorite color is and what my dog's name is. I may have exaggerated the last couple, but he is happy to see me nonetheless.

He brings my drink and a bowl of the soup-of-the-day, which regardless of the name, all tastes the same. It is a blend of tomato, spinach, broccoli, potato, and whatever else is available that day, which somehow tastes wonderful. After nearly every spoonful, he returns to check on my progress. It is bordering on annoying. As I'm eating and looking out the window, a couple of vans and two cars all stop across the street in the middle of the road. I point to the assemblage and tell the waiter the police would soon be breaking that meeting up.

He replies, "I don't think so, sir. That's the IRA and in these parts, no one, not even the police, messes with the IRA." I thought the IRA had disbanded years ago. I had no idea they still operated and was actually thrilled to witness an actual IRA meeting, as bland as it seemed to be. One older man got out of his car and walked to the nearest van. The van window rolled down and as clear as the sun on a cloudless day, I see Ailin sitting there waiting to talk to the older man.

They say a few words, then all four vehicles drive away. I'm sure it is Ailin. Just as I am sure I have no idea what I've just seen, or what it all means. Or, if the waiter knows what he is talking about when he says they are the IRA. But, it is all very interesting.

I was only gone from Dungloe less than two hours. I returned and made my rounds waving and saying hello in the businesses Ailin owned (which was nearly the whole town). I was looking forward to my evening meeting with Ailen, unsure if I should bring up my seeing him today or not. First, he'd want to know why I was in Burtonport; second, he might just tell me to mind my own business and stay out of his. Either way, bringing it up was probably not a good idea. I'll keep my mouth shut.

We each ordered a plain, which for you non-Irish, means a Guinness. As usual he was quiet and also as usual, I waited until he was ready to discuss anything. After half a pint, he looked at me and said, "Why were you in Burtonport this morning?" Uh oh! Before I could make anything up, but not before beads of sweat popped out on my face, he said, "I saw you walk in the pub on Center Street. If you lie to me again Mark, I'll ask you to leave. I must be able to trust you. I told you that before."

So I told him the truth. I went there because I wanted a place to bank that was not his. I also didn't want people knowing my business. If he didn't like it or was offended by that, then he could let me go. He took another sip and said, "I'd have given you a safe deposit box here for free. No questions asked." How did he know I got a safe deposit box? Then he said, "You know you can trust me, don't you Mark?"

Without thinking, and quite stupidly, I responded, "Well Ailin, you ARE in the IRA." As soon as I said it, I knew . . . I KNEW . . . I shouldn't have. He put his pint down and stared at me. I stared at the table.

He finally said, "Mark, it's better not to know things sometimes."

Now, I taught myself a good lesson, never miss a good chance to shut up!

We each finished our drinks and sat there. The waitress knew enough not to come near our table. Finally he said, "You have nothing to fear from me. I'm your friend. If I wanted to harm you, I'd have told your wife and her new husband where you are a long time ago." What? Huh? Oh my God!!! How does he? How could he possibly?

We continued to sit in silence. I had no idea what to say. What could I say that he didn't already know? Sensing my awkwardness and uncomfortable demeanor, he explained exactly what I was thinking. "Yes, I'm in the IRA. No, we're not dangerous. Those days are over. Do I want the British out of Northern Ireland? Yes. Will we hurt anyone to achieve those ends? No, not physically anyway. We use other tactics now. We're smarter than we used to be."

He continued, "I want you to understand this Mark. Wrong is wrong, even if everyone is doing it. And, right is right, even if no one is doing it." I nodded. There was no way on God's green earth I was going to say anything. He motioned for the waitress to bring me another plain. He then got up to leave and said, "See you tomorrow, and by the way, I think you should ask Claire out."

6

I LEARNED, quite by accident, that Ailin was a very successful author in Ireland. He has written a couple of history books about Ireland that are used in many schools and colleges throughout the country. They are not used in Great Britain because Ailin's books are generally anti-British and are slanted towards his Irish readership. That's why they're so popular. He has also written a couple of novels that sell extremely well in Ireland, since they promote Irish pride. None of his books are kind to Britain and their history with Ireland.

The next evening I brought up this subject with Ailin and told him how impressed I was with his authorship. He explained to me that his books are the only reason Dungloe has survived. The town had virtually closed up, the businesses had nearly all failed. The bank had also closed and only the pub remained operable because nearly all the people were drinking themselves to death. After Ailin's first history book became successful, he took most of the proceeds he made and started investing in the town.

He opened the restaurant, then the bank and made sure the pub was financially stable. The two novels enabled him to open up additional businesses and employ even more people. The last history book was so overwhelmingly popular that Ailin was set financially for the rest of his life. So what did he do with his money? He invested in his town, in his country, in his fellow men. He saved Dungloe.

He quite openly explained to me that nearly all of his businesses in town struggle to break even. Only the bank, the pub and the restaurant are financially secure. He seemed in such a talkative mood that I really ventured out on a limb and asked him how he knew of my past. How does he know of my ex-wife, her new husband and everything else?

"Mark," he said, "I don't do things carelessly or lightly. I do my homework, from writing books, or investing in businesses, or hiring people. I knew of you the first day you arrived, but I only investigated after you spoke to me. I knew from our first conversation that you weren't our normal pub patron. I knew there was something about you. Something I needed to find out. So I did. How I did that is of no concern to you, other than to know I have contacts in many places.

I like people with depth. I like people with emotions. I like people with a strong mind, an interesting mind, a twisted mind, and also people that can make me smile. Mark, time decides who you meet in your life. Your heart decides who you want in your life and your behavior decides who stays in your life. Life itself simply has a way of working out, just when you start to believe it never will. I think this applies to us both, don't you?"

This was the first time I was pretty sure Ailin was the smartest man in the world.

I continued on with my daily duties: ordering this, fixing that, settling disputes, filling in when needed. Anything Ailin needed to be done. I had tried my best to avoid going into the restaurant however, but they called one morning and told me they were nearly out of bacon. Being out of bacon is probably the third worst thing that could happen in Ireland. Being out of Guinness and then potatoes being first and second.

I wasn't particularly looking forward to meeting Claire again, but duty called. They were indeed all but out of bacon and couldn't wait for the weekly delivery the next morning. I had to go to the butcher's shop and bring some back immediately for the lunch crowd. On my return, Claire met me in the kitchen and asked if I'd be having lunch in the restaurant now. Well, I guess so, I can't keep avoiding her forever.

I found a table near the back by myself and she came over to take my order. I could tell she was either mad at me, or mad at something. I wasn't sure which. Since she didn't bring me a menu I wasn't exactly sure what to do. Then she spoke. "I'll have you know sir, in no uncertain terms at all, I do not want to date you. I'll do my job here and be as pleasant as I can, but I will not go out with you!"

I was stunned. I didn't know how to answer that, but she just stood there staring at me, expecting a response, I assumed. "Well miss, if I'm not mistaken, I have not asked you out on a date, nor do I have any intention of ever asking you out."

Her eyes widened and her complexion fully flushed. She then frowned deeply and said, "Oscar Wilde was right when he said, 'A gentleman is one who never hurts anyone's feelings unintentionally.' Your lunch will be right out."

I didn't know if Oscar Wilde actually said that or not, or even know exactly what it meant. But I did know that I hadn't ordered any lunch and wondered what she would bring me. After fifteen minutes of waiting, I found out what she was bringing me—nothing. She never came back, so I eventually got up and left and went to the pub for lunch. What a weird day.

Back at the pub I sat at the bar and ordered a sandwich while talking to the bartender. He was a fellow that baffled me to no end. His name is Ruaraidh, but pronounced like Rory, and he's a known drunk. I'm baffled as to why Ailin has this drunkard as his bartender. Ailin doesn't make careless mistakes, and as I know, he checks everything out.

I like Ruaraidh, but I don't understand how someone can start drinking mid-morning and drink throughout the day and continue existing. And, all he ever talks about is drinking. He knows everything there is to know about beer, wine, whiskey and lets you know that he does. As I sit eating my lunch, he ambles over to me and starts discussing the latest batch of Irish whiskey they'd received. According to him it is an excellent vintage. I have no clue, and didn't answer him.

He said, "You do drink don't you Mark?"

"Yes, Ruaraidh, I do. But not all the time, certainly not in the middle of the day."

He has the most quizzical look on his face as he replied, "I feel sorry for people who don't drink. When they wake up in the morning, that's as good as they're going to feel all day." Rather than try to respond to that, I just nod and keep eating. Ruaraidh goes to the other end of the bar, but keeps looking back at me. I knew he wasn't finished and soon he stumbles back to me and says, "Dinosaurs had no beer. How did that work out?" Well, you can't argue with logic.

That evening as Ailin and I sat sipping a beer, I asked him about Ruaraidh. He sat his glass down and took a deep breath and looked up at the ceiling. I starting thinking to myself that I should've just kept quiet. He finally looked back at me and said, "Well, I guess I do owe you an explanation, since you're working with him. It's obvious he's a hopeless drunk. But he's honest and he doesn't get sloppy drunk and pass out. He just likes to drink. He's also my wife's brother."

Wow! I didn't know Ailin was married. He'd never talked of a wife, or wore a wedding ring, or made any reference whatsoever of being married. I know he lives in the apartment above the bar. I see him going up there every evening and I NEVER see anyone else go up there with him. I was extremely puzzled. But, fortunately for me, I've learned my lesson to be quiet and wait. If he wants to tell me something, he will.

He finally looked up from his drink and said, "Yes, I'm married; and no, we don't live together. She lives out of town, by the ocean, quite alone and apparently very happy." And before I could even think of the next question I would've asked, not that I would have, he continued, "I, on the other hand, am not happy. However, I made a huge mistake that I imagine I'll keep paying for as long as I live."

Ailin talked longer than he'd ever spoken with me before. He seemed relieved to tell the entire story, even his past transgressions and the pain he lives with. Several years earlier Ailin and his pals had traveled to Galway for a hurling match between Galway and his local Donegal Club. His boys had won and they were all out getting thoroughly soused after the game at a local club in Galway. A young lass, apparently very attractive, well built and scantily clad, began making advances towards Ailin, and his senses, being dulled with drink, temporarily abandoned him. Unfortunately, his so-called friends uploaded a video on a social media website of Ailin and the young lass deep in the throes of passion.

Ailin's wife saw the video. He moved out the next day and was told she'd let him know when, if ever, he was forgiven. According to Ailin, that was 4 years, 11 months and 22 days ago. I feel certain he also knew the hours and minutes as painfully well.

When he finished this sad story, he looked at me and said, "Mark, there are nights when the wolves are silent and only the moon howls. That was one of those nights." Then he got up from the table to leave, but first turned back to me and said, "I heard Claire turned you down the other day, but don't worry, women are meant to be loved, not to be understood." And he walked upstairs.

Claire turned me down?!? What???

7

THE WEATHER CHANGED OVERNIGHT. The new day was entirely cloudless, warm and beautiful. It was amazing how sunny days changed everything in Ireland. People were smiling; flowers seemed to respond with brilliant colors, and the various shades of green were something even Dali or Picasso could not have painted. Sometimes I think the Irish forget the sun and how it feels and how it makes them feel. I mentioned this to Ailin this morning as we sat outside and sipped our tea and coffee together. He nodded, then almost as if speaking to the world itself, he said, "And still after all this time Mark, the sun never looks at the earth and says, 'You owe me.' It just continues to light up the sky."

I wanted to bring up this whole thing about Claire and her "turning me down," but Ailin received a call and had to run. I had no idea who he was talking to, but he abruptly ended the call with, "Life's under no obligation to give us what we expect!" If he'd had a regular phone instead of his cell phone, I'm sure he'd have slammed it down. I asked if everything was alright. He said, "Mark, I truly want to help the helpless, but I don't want to help the clueless!" With that, he got in his car, went straight through the roundabout and headed out of town.

Now that the folks in town were getting to know me better, they each started requesting my help with things. Can I do this or that? Can I speak with Ailin about something, can I fill in for them whilst they take care of some personal business? I didn't really mind actually; it was still new to me and I enjoyed meeting everyone. But this thing with Claire still bothered me—it shouldn't have, but it did. I made my mind up I was going to clear the air between us and tell her to stop announcing that she had "turned me down."

I waited till after the lunch crowd had thinned out before I visited the restaurant where she worked. When I walked in she was still cleaning off tables, but turned to me and said, "I'm sorry, but we're nearly out of everything. Why don't you try back tomorrow?"

Stay calm, I told myself. Don't let her get to you, I told myself. Be the adult here, I told myself. However, I didn't listen to myself. I said, "I'm not here for lunch, but I would like a word with you if you don't mind."

She frowned and replied, "Well, since you're Ailin's boy, I guess I have no choice but to talk to you."

See why I didn't listen to myself? I tried to take a deep breath and said, "I am not Ailin's boy! And I want you to stop telling people that I asked you out on a date. You and I both know that never happened, and it never will happen."

"But you want it to. And trust me 'boy' I would never go out with an American if you were the last American on earth!"

"Well let me tell you something missy, I wouldn't date a plain-Jane, unattractive, simple, lying Amish girl if you were the last woman on earth." At this point, I felt I was in full control of my emotions.

Claire stared at me and then said, "I don't care what you say, or how often you beg. I'm not going out with you. And why can't you ever be happy like everyone else? No girl wants to date someone who's always mad and crazy."

"I AM HAPPY." I screamed, "But you're making me crazy."

"Well, too bad. I'm not going out with you. Goodbye."

And with that, she turned and walked back into the kitchen. I wanted to punch something, until I turned around and saw an old man and old woman silently staring at me from the corner. I said, "Good day to you."

And I started out the front door when the old man spoke, "I think she likes you son."

Don't! Don't even think about it Paul, or Mark, or whatever my name is. Walk out, go home, or better yet, go back to the pub and have a drink. Maybe two.

I did go back to the pub, but not to drink, just to calm down and figure out why I was allowing this woman to get me so upset. I could understand if a pretty girl had rebuffed my advances. That happens to every guy. But Claire? I don't find her attractive, I don't want to date her and I would really like to not speak to her ever again. As I was sitting at the bar thinking, Ruaraidh came over and asked if I wanted a drink. "No, I don't. And why do you always ask me if I want a drink?"

He had this quizzical look on his face and said, "I guess because you're sitting at a bar in the pub." The first sensible thing he'd ever said.

"I'm sorry Ruaraidh, I'm just having a bad day. I had an argument with someone at the restaurant that really irked me."

"Oh," he said, "Claire turned you down again? She turned me down once as well." I could not believe what I was hearing. Why in the world does everyone in this town think I asked the homeliest, Amish girl this side of Pennsylvania out on a date? So I asked Ruaraidh why he would think that? Who told him I had asked Claire out?

"Everybody knows it," he replied, "don't feel too bad about it. She's pretty picky. I had no chance with her."

"You asked Claire out on a date?"

"Yeah, but she wouldn't go."

I thought to myself that at least she's not entirely stupid, but said to Ruaraidh, "What did she say when you asked her out?"

"She just said 'No!' So I asked her why and then she said, 'I wasn't born with enough middle fingers to let you know how I feel about you Ruaraidh!'"

So, here we are, Ruaraidh and me both turned down by the same girl. One of us because he's a drunk and an oaf, the other one of us because he NEVER ASKED HER OUT IN THE FIRST PLACE!!!

I spent the rest of the afternoon doing busy work, answering phone calls and ordering supplies. All the stuff Ailin hired me to do so he could go off to do wherever it is he goes off to do every day. Where does he go off to anyway? Sometimes I'm a little too nosy for my own good. I couldn't stop wondering about this now. What does a man with a lot of money and power, who's in the IRA, do all day? Where does he go? And, what's he up to?

I decided I would tactfully and cautiously broach that subject this evening when he returned, and hope I didn't piss him off. As we sat sipping our first Guinness of the night, he was quiet as usual, happy to relax and unwind after doing God knows what all day. Finally, I couldn't stand it any longer and said, "Ailin, I'm curious, what do you do all day when you're gone? Is there anything I can help you with?" I thought this might be a good idea, to offer my help, while not seeming to be too nosey.

He thought for a few moments, then looked up and replied, "There's a wide gap between people knowing what I actually do, and really believing that I still do that, and wondering what it is that I really do." I pretended to understand what he meant. He then added, "Mark, if you're looking for something else to do, why don't you try fishing. You might enjoy it."

"Maybe I'll try that Ailin. Thanks. Do you do a lot of fishing yourself?"

Again, he took a few moments before he spoke, then he said, "No, I don't. Fishing is actually pretty boring, unless you catch an actual fish, and then it's disgusting." He had a slight smile on his face as he rose to go upstairs. I wish I knew if he was smiling at that comment he made, or at me.

Later that same night, as I sat and listened to the enchanting music of the locals, an extremely attractive woman entered the pub. I hadn't seen her before, but she seemed to know everyone there and spoke to most of them. Ruaraidh fumbled all over himself trying to bring her a glass of wine, which he spilled on the way to her table. She then told him she rather have a plain, which seemed to ease his anxiety a bit.

She eventually went to a large table full of older people and sat with them listening to the music. Obviously, they were all well acquainted with each other. After a few minutes I ambled up to the bar, as unobtrusively as possible, and finally got Ruaraidh's attention. Any other day he would be fumbling and drooling all over me, now I can't get him to come near me. When he finally does come over, he brings me another pint, even though my current pint is over half full.

When he finally shuts up, I ask him who the attractive woman is that just came in the bar. He looks around and says, "What attractive woman?" I could not believe this. There were about six fat teenaged girls, five old women, three middle-aged spinsters, of which none had any teeth that I could see, and about five or six little girls running around. Then there was this beauty sitting there amongst them all, shining like a light house in the middle of a foggy night, and Ruaraidh says, "What attractive woman?"

I turned to point at her and say "That one you oaf, are you blind?" But as I pointed, she looked over at me as my finger was pointing directly at her. Our eyes met for just an instant and she turned away back to her conversation.

Anyway, Ruaraidh knew then who I was referring to and said, "Oh, that's Ailin's wife, Mairead."

Then I asked a dumb question, "Are you sure?"

Next, it was Ruaraidh's turn to ask a dumb question, "Of course I'm sure, do you think I'm daft?"

As I was trying to connect the dots here, someone tapped me on the shoulder and said, "Excuse me." I turned around and almost melted as I looked into the prettiest blue eyes I'd ever seen. Mairead then looked at Ruaraidh and said, "Do you mind if I have a moment alone with Mark?" What was he going to say, no?

She looked at me and smiled and if she hadn't been Ailin's wife, I'm not sure what I'd have done. She was certainly one of the most stunning women I'd ever seen. Something about her eyes and the bone structure of her face made her extraordinary. "I hope I'm not interrupting anything important."

"No, it's a pleasure to meet you." I said. I truly didn't know what else TO say.

She continued, "I've heard good things about you. I hope you're enjoying your stay here in our little town. I know Ailin loves having you here. Don't let him get into too much trouble, if you don't mind."

I tried to compose myself and said, "I'll do the best I can, but I think Ailin can take care of himself."

Before I could think of anything else to say, she said, "It's nice to meet you Mark. It is Mark isn't it?" And before I could lie to her, she said, "We'll have plenty of time to talk later. Oh, and don't give up on Claire, keep asking her, she may change her mind." And with that, she turned and swayed back to her table.

Is there anybody in this entire country who doesn't think Claire turned me down for a date that I never asked her on? As they say here in Ireland—Jesus, Mary, and Joseph!

8

I DIDN'T SEE AILIN that evening. He never showed up in the pub, although I did see his car parked out front. I couldn't wait to actually meet with him in the morning and tell him I'd met his wife, Mairead. But again, I was disappointed. Ailin didn't show up for our morning tea and coffee meeting either. This was pretty strange. During the day I had to send Ruaraidh home. He stumbled once too often and spilled one too many drinks. He mildly protested, but I think he was happy to actually go home and sleep it off.

Ailin finally appeared after 7:00 that evening, looking tired and a bit worn. He came up to the bar and asked where Ruaraidh was, and when I told him he just shook his head and apologized. He sat at the end of the bar so he and I could talk in relative privacy, which wasn't much of an issue, since everyone knew never to disturb Ailin. I reviewed the last two days, as mundane as it was, and finished my report by telling him I'd met his wife. This was the only time he looked up from his Guinness.

I told him she'd come into the pub and had spoken to me and that I found her very attractive and especially personable. He didn't respond and neither did I. Finally, after he finished his drink, he stood up and looked at me and said as he was leaving, "Mark, wisdom has two parts; first, having a lot to say. And, second, not saying it."

It sounded very prophetic. I'm not exactly sure what it applied to at that moment—but it seemed very appropriate.

Later that evening, as I served drinks and listened to the nightly music, one of the fiddle players came to the bar to order drinks for the musicians who were taking a short break. He was about 45 years old I'm guessing, hadn't shaved in a few days, and apparently hadn't changed clothes either. He was fairly short, a little heavy and had these stubby, little fat fingers. I'd never noticed them before until he paid me for the drinks. I wondered how he could play a violin so well with those stubby little fingers. He knew me, but I didn't know his name, nor anything else about him.

When he came back to pick up the last of the pints, I told him how much I enjoyed the music and asked what his name was. I couldn't understand what he said. He sensed that and tried to pronounce it again slowly, which only confused me further. I simply nodded and he smiled. I asked him where he learned to play so well. He said, "I've always played. The fiddle and the guitar."

I continued, "I've heard you play both, you're fantastic. But how did you learn to play? Did you take lessons?"

"Lessons?" He said, "Heavens no. I just play."

"But how did you learn to play?"

He cocked his head a little, as though I was speaking a foreign language and replied, "We don't need lessons lad. We just play."

Okay, enough was enough. I smiled and said, "Great. Well, I certainly enjoy it. Keep it up." I'm pretty sure he thought I was completely daft, or from America.

The next morning is once again sunny and brilliant. Whatever the temperature and humidity and dew point is, it's perfect. Ailin came down and we sat outside and enjoyed each other's company in peace, as we sipped our hot drinks. I came to understand that I shouldn't talk unless I can improve the silence. As we deliberated, trying to decide whether or not to have a second cup, Ailin turned to me and said, "I think you should know, there was some news about you in America today." He could not have surprised me more if he'd told me Ruaraidh just won the Nobel Prize for literature.

It was easy for him to see I was completely stunned and speechless. So he started to explain, "When you appeared here in Dungloe that first day and we learned you were going to stay, I began to make inquiries." He paused and checked to make sure his cup of tea was completely empty. "It was obvious you weren't who you said you were, just as it was obvious to everyone that you are from America."

I stopped him and asked, "When you say 'everyone,' exactly who else knows I'm from America besides you?"

He then did something he'd never done around me, he rolled his eyes and said, "Everyone Mark. From Ruaraidh on down, or up, as the case may be."

I said, "You mean no one believed my story? I thought everyone else accepted it."

"Look Mark, geographically speaking, Ireland may be a medium-sized rural island that is slowly and steadily being consumed by sheep, but we aren't stupid or naïve. Most of us anyway. No one believed that cockamamie story of yours, but being Irish, no one really cared either. We accept you for who you are and how you treat us and others. I only found it strange that an American would choose to settle in Dungloe. By himself, with a strange and wild story. Why not just tell the truth, unless you have something to hide?"

He let this settle in, then continued "And being in my position, I needed to find out exactly who you are and who you may be working for: the British, my competitors, the British, the English, or the British? As you can see, I'm a bit paranoid of our neighbors."

I looked him directly in the eye and said, "Ailin, I'm not working for anyone, least of all the British. I hope you believe that."

"Oh, I believe it. I checked you out first, but I thoroughly believe you now."

Next, I had to ask the question that had been on my mind since the beginning, "Exactly how did you check me out?"

He didn't hesitate, "It took a little work but we, meaning my team and I, knew you were from America. We narrowed it down by your accent. Certainly you weren't from the North or the Midwest and probably not the West coast either. Your slight drawl made us pretty sure it was from somewhere in the South.

We then Googled each state in the American south and asked for 'missing persons' within the last couple of months. The fourth state we looked at, North Carolina, had a Paul Alfred, whose name we didn't recognize, but whose picture we did. It was you. I then called your home town, Winston-Salem, and found the number of a private detective I could hire quite reasonably. I told him what I wanted and in a couple of days he called back with more than I expected. We knew about your business, your life, your history, and most importantly, I think, your ex-wife and her new husband."

"I don't want you to worry about anything. This investigator seemed trustworthy and I feel very confident he will never divulge any information about my inquiries."

I asked who the investigator was, in the slim chance I may have known him. After all, Winston-Salem is not a large city. He told me, "His name is Desmond Jones. He was familiar with your name because it was in the papers that you'd disappeared. But he didn't know you. He was a funny man, not in the comical sense, but in that he was almost rude to the point where I nearly hung up the phone on him. But after a few more questions, I could tell he knew what he was doing and could be trusted. He's on a retainer that pays him to notify me of any news concerning you. If there is nothing, then I won't hear from him again, but I don't want to close the door just yet."

I sat there shaking my head in disbelief as he continued, "The reason I'm bringing this up is because he called me yesterday with some news. Your name was in the newspaper again." Incredulously, I asked why. He said, "Apparently your ex-wife and her husband have petitioned the court to declare you legally dead so they can collect the life insurance on you."

I found this extremely interesting, since I had no life insurance policy whatsoever. I told Ailin this and he replied, "Well apparently you do, a large one, in the sum of two million dollars."

This should not have surprised me at all, having known what Gina and Charles were capable of. But it did! I looked at Ailin in despair and disbelief hoping for something, anything to quiet my angst. He continued, "Apparently, in America, they have to wait a full year to declare someone 'legally dead.' So your ex cannot immediately cash in on your untimely demise my friend. But she will eventually, unless . . ."

"Unless what?" I said, hoping for a miracle.

"Unless you go back over there, prove you're still alive and foil their plans," he said. "Or, stay here and let them collect the money, and live your new life without fear of them trying to hunt you down and make good on all the debt you left them. Your decision, my friend."

"What would you do, Ailin? Just let the cheating scoundrels get away with the two million?"

Ailin took a couple of deep breaths, then looked at me and said, "Mark, that's your decision. But I have the feeling that you didn't come this far to only come this far."

I couldn't decide whether to start screaming, crying or drinking. And at this point in the morning, I needed something quite a bit stronger than coffee, but a little less than cocaine. While I contemplated my positon, Ailin texted someone, and within one minute a van pulled up out front and as he rose he looked back at me and said, "Oh, I do have some good news. Mairead told me that you and Claire might be getting together after all." Before I could comprehend what he'd just said, he was in the van and off.

Unbelievable!

After several minutes, I felt composed enough to walk back inside the pub. All this news was quite unnerving. Certainly some people believed my story of how I arrived in Dungloe. I know Ruaraidh did. I went to the bar near him and asked how he felt today and if I could help with anything. He didn't answer at first and I was wondering if he actually was okay. Finally, he said he was fine, but didn't want to talk about it. "Talk about what?" I said.

"Whatever you and Ailin were whispering about outside. I know it was about me."

"No it wasn't Ruaraidh, we were discussing business matters and some personal information— nothing about you."

He looked quite relieved and said, "I know Ailin thinks I'm craiceailte, but I do my job!"

I had no idea what "craiceailte" meant, but I could guess. "Trust me Ruaraidh, we were not talking about you at all. In fact, I was explaining to Ailin where I'm from." Ruaraidh stared at me, I stared back at him. Then I said, "You remember where I'm from don't you Ruaraidh?"

"Umm, yes Mark. Whatever you say."

"No, Ruaraidh, not whatever I say. Where do you think I'm from?" He sort of mumbled something, then said he had to get back to work, even though there were no customers here yet. "Ruaraidh," I demanded, "tell me where you think I'm from!"

He walked back over to me and said, "Do you want your version, or do you want the truth?"

You cannot be serious! Even Ruaraidh knows my story is a lie! What a depressing, disgusting day it's been, and it's not even 10:00 in the morning.

9

BACK IN THE USA, Gina and Charles knew Paul wasn't dead. They soon figured out he was in hiding when his car found at a used car dealership in Norfolk, Virginia. However, they had no idea where he was or if he would ever show up in their lives again. But Charles, being the Charles he was, saw the advantage in this whole scenario. He soon concocted the whole idea of the fake life insurance policy and had it approved by an ever-greedy Gina.

Charles was in the midst of a court proceeding where he was defending an independent insurance agent who had been accused of misappropriating funds from his customers for his own personal use. The man was guilty as sin and had been using the monthly premiums from his customers to buy cars, boats and trips, all in the vain attempt to impress the much younger girlfriend he left his wife of 20 years for. This man's problem was that now he had no money left to pay Charles and was on the verge of being assigned a court appointed attorney, probably someone just out of law school who didn't have a clue how to play the game.

Charles and this other weasel soon developed a plan whereby the insurance agent would draw up the two million dollar policy and have it back-dated to several months before Paul disappeared. Charles would then represent the weasel pro bono and, through his crooked contacts in the judicial system, he would negotiate the most attractive terms possible for his client. The weasel would still be guilty. But he would only spend a minimal amount of time in a low-security, country club type of prison. Then, after an appropriate period of time, he'd be released with little or no publicity. Absolutely the best deal possible for the weasel and a two million dollar payday for Gina and Charles.

The only glitch in this scheme would be if Paul somehow reappeared in their lives and ruined the entire show. This was why Charles had a private detective working all clues and traces of anything related to Paul. So far, he'd found nothing except for his abandoned car in Norfolk and a bartender in a seedy pub who "thinks" he may have seen someone looking like Paul talking to some freighter people. But, he would keep investigating.

10

THE THOUGHTS OF GINA, the slut, and Charles, the snake, getting two million dollars totally consumed my thinking. I could, if I chose, go back over there and ruin the entire scheme of theirs. But certainly I would be in some sort of trouble legally. Or I could simply forget it and let them have the money and live here free and easy. The question being, "Can I forget it?" The answer being, "I don't know."

I was happy to see Ailin again that evening. Even though I was still wondering what he did all day, I now needed his advice and counseling to help me through this crisis of mine even more. We sat and he ordered a couple of pints. I knew to always wait until he was ready to talk, but it was killing me to wait. I fidgeted. I cracked my knuckles. I shifted positions. I was begging him to talk to me. Silently, of course.

He finally looked up and said, "What?" That's all I needed. For the next twenty minutes I reviewed my problem and all my options, even some new options I dreamed up. He sat there and sipped and listened. When I had no more to say, I finished by telling him this was how I saw things. He motioned for the waitress to bring him another plain, and said, "Mark, it's not what you look at that matters, it's what you see. My advice is to not look back. You're not going that way. The slut and the snake, as you describe them, aren't so much AGAINST you as they are FOR themselves."

Okay, how do I respond to that when I know he's right? He then looked at me and smiled saying, "A slut you say?"

Now I smiled and replied, "Well, by slut, I mean she has the morals of a man."

We both laughed, then he said, "And her husband is a low-down dog and a snake as well?"

"No Ailin, a dog will look down when he's done wrong. A snake will look you right in the eye."

We both smiled, we both sipped, and we were both silent. Ailin then rose to leave and said, "There are good days and there are bad days, and this is one of them." He went up the steps to his apartment, quite alone as always. I continued to sit there, contemplating my life and wondering what in the world he meant by that last statement.

Ailin and I met for coffee and tea in the morning. I had a frightful and restless night trying to sleep, while futilely reliving the past day's events. After two cups of silence, Ailin texted someone and a car appeared out front. He rose, looked down at me and said, "Mark, the magic of Ireland is all around, you just have to believe."

I went back inside and finished up some invoicing and ordering. Taking care of several other menial tasks while Ailin was off doing God knows what. I thought I might be able to trick Ruaraidh into telling me something of Ailin's activities. Well, I knew I could trick him; it wouldn't be that difficult. But I was unsure if he knew anything more than me of what Ailin did all day.

When Ruaraidh came in, I started making small talk with him again. It wasn't easy. I told him I'd like to have his email address so I could correspond with him and send him stuff. He frowned a little and replied, "I don't do technology junk."

"You don't have an email address, Ruaraidh?"

He looked hard at me said, "I don't have anything with technology."

I believed him. I didn't understand him, but I believed him. I couldn't let it go, however, and continued, "So you're not dazzled and inspired by computers and such?"

He snarled back, "I will not be impressed with technology until I can download actual wine and beer."

He had a point. Time to change the subject. "Ruaraidh, I was thinking of helping Ailin all day tomorrow. Will you be okay here by yourself?" (The best lie I could think of)

"Of course I'll be alright, do you think I'm stupid?" Don't answer that, just don't answer it. And before I could, he continued, "And, anyway, Ailin doesn't need your help. He and the boys get along fine without you."

"I'm sure they do, but everyone can use an extra hand from time to time, right?" C'mon Ruaraidh, answer. Say something. Give me something. But no, he turned and started wiping down tables.

Another uneventful day passed, except that I saw Claire, the Amish girl, walking down the street and I quickly crossed to the other side to avoid her and her sarcastic temperament. When I had crossed over, I looked towards her for an instant and I swear if I could have read lips, I'm sure she was saying, "No."

That evening, I filled Ailin in on all the day's non-events and activities. All he did was nod and sip his nightly Guinness. When I completed my rundown of the mundane, he said, "So I understand you're going to help me and the boys tomorrow." Oh crap! That tattletale Ruaraidh. Before I could think of anything, he said, "I appreciate your sincerity and I know you're curious about what I do. But, Mark, very few of us are what we seem. It would be in your best interest to channel your curiosity towards more enlightening subjects."

I took this as an invitation so I asked him, "Okay, tell me what happened that night in Galway when you were videotaped with the girl? Somehow, something like that doesn't fit with your personality. And, quite honestly, I don't see how you could actually do something like that to your wife. Mairead has to be better than any floozy you could have picked up in a pub."

At first I thought he might punch me. Then I thought for sure he'd tell me to shut up and mind my own business. But he didn't do either. Instead, he explained: "Nothing ever goes away until it teaches us what we need to know. I learned a very hard lesson that night, Mark. Sometimes your friends aren't who you think they are, and even more importantly, the trouble with trouble, is that it always starts out as fun. Our hurling club had just beaten Galway, and we NEVER beat Galway. We were all happy and wanted to have a few drinks in the local pub to celebrate.

As you know, I enjoy a drink or two, but seldom more than that. I've never been drunk since one night when I was seventeen, experimenting with Irish whiskey. I got sick, threw up and passed out on a curb in front of the church. My parents were not amused. I made the vow then that I'd never lose control of myself again through drink. And I never did till that night.

There are varying degrees of what I know and what I think I know that happened that night. Certainly, the pure and simple truth is rarely pure and never simple. I know, at least I remember, only having two pints of Guinness that night. My next memory is waking the next morning with a terrible headache. I have no recollection of the girl or anything else. I'm not denying it happened, because I've seen the tape. I'm only saying that I don't remember it.

What I've learned since then was that one of our mates, who I thought was a fairly new, but trusted friend, was not what he seemed. You see Mark, the British do not like me at all; in fact, they hate my guts."

I had to interrupt and ask why the British hated him so much.

"Because every book I've written, both the history books and the novels, have not only told the truth about their exploitation of Ireland and our people, but have at times embellished their deeds negatively—especially in the novels. They don't like it and they especially don't like the idea that all my books are best sellers and are spreading throughout Europe, where anti-British sentiments are vocal anyway.

My newest friend went to the bar to bring drinks back to us that night, and there were no women at our table at that point. He handed me my pint and told a joke about a Derryman and Ulsterman and that's the last thing I remember. I woke up the next morning in a bedroom upstairs with this raging headache and all my mates nowhere in sight. I had no idea what happened.

I found a bus and travelled back to Dungloe, ashamed of my actions. Getting soused and passing out was not something I was proud of. Not till I got home and rang my mates did I know anything of the girl or that my so-called friend had videotaped me with the girl. It went downhill from there. Mairead received an email of the video from an untraceable email account and headlines in the papers stated, 'Famous Author Caught Cheating!'

Mark, I am 100% certain, my so-called friend was working for the British and put something in my drink that night to render me unconscious. He's the one who brought me the pint. He's the one who videotaped the incident. And he's the only one who disappeared and hasn't been heard from since that night. The British were trying to embarrass me and hurt me in front of my wife and countrymen. They did a good job of it.

Of course Mairead was furious, hurt and embarrassed by the whole affair. I don't blame her. I tried to explain what happened, but all she would say was that I tried to blame everything on the British. I think it might've been better if I'd just said, 'yes, I got drunk and made a huge mistake.' But in blaming the Brits, she thinks I've not assumed responsibility for my actions. She's hurt and I don't know how to undo that hurt and make things right again. I love her with all my heart and soul, and I always will."

I did not know what to say, but to prove I'd indeed learned something from Ailin, I kept quiet. However, I absolutely knew at that moment in time that I was indeed going to help Ailin and the boys, and that an adventure was definitely going to happen.

11

TWO DAYS LATER, at the butcher's shop, I run into Mairead quite by accident. I'm certainly not going to bring up any of the business with her husband. As before, she is very pleasant and extremely attractive. Without question, she is the prettiest woman in Dungloe, or maybe all of Ireland, that I've seen. She asks how I am adjusting to Dungloe and small town Irish culture. She says, "It must be a huge change for an American used to a completely different lifestyle."

I honestly reply that except for the weather, I am thoroughly enjoying it.

She laughs and says, "Don't knock the weather in Ireland, without it, 90% of us couldn't start a conversation." As we both laugh, I ask her if she's ever visited my country. She replies, "America, Mark, is not a country. It's a world." Even though she didn't actually answer my question, I absolutely know what she means. And I also know not to repeat the question. I am learning.

She asks me if I've travelled elsewhere in Europe, and since my cover is now blown, I honestly tell her no, but I'd like to someday soon. I ask her which countries she

prefers, "aside from heaven on earth right here, of
course."

She seems to enjoy that comment and then tells me,
"Well, Mark, actually in heaven the food is Italian, the
police are British, the engineers are German, the lovers
are French and everything is organized by the Swiss.
However, if you make a wrong turn and end up in Hell,
the food is British, the police are German, the engineers
are French, the lovers are Swiss and everything is
organized by the Italians."

She actually giggles as she tells me this. Is there anything
more alluring than a beautiful woman looking at you and
giggling with you over some amusing remark? Between
her humor and her looks I am completely smitten. It
didn't hurt either that her blouse is probably unbuttoned
one button too many. Looking at cleavage is like looking
into the sun. You don't stare at it; it's too risky. You just
get a sense of it and then you look away. It was hard to
look away.

"Well, I must be running, Mark. Plenty of errands to
finish up. Please let me know if there's anything I can do
to make your stay here in Dungloe more pleasant. Oh, and
Claire mentioned you spoke to her on the street the other
day in passing. Don't get discouraged, I think she might
change her mind one day soon. Just keep asking her. Bye,
Mark."

I could have rebutted that last statement. I should've set
the record straight that I DID NOT talk to Claire, nor ask

her out, on the street the other day. I should've protested the whole thing. But watching Mairead walk away from me was much more pleasant than anything else I could think of at the moment. Wow, and did she just tell me to let her know if there's anything she can do to make my stay here in Dungloe more pleasant?

Why couldn't Mairead be single and available instead of that psycho, Amish woman who keeps telling people I'm asking her out? Such is life. Time for me to drink some coffee and pretend that I know what I'm doing.

After I make my rounds I go back to the pub to have that second cup of morning coffee. Ruaraidh is sitting at a table by himself with an empty glass in front of him. I look at him and say, "Have you been drinking already?"

Without moving a muscle he replies, "Why, do I have an ugly girl sitting next to me?" Sometimes, it's hard to be a nice human being. This was one of those times. Ruaraidh has two things in his favor: one, he's Mairead's brother, and two, he has no idea what he's doing and he's very good at it.

Inexplicably, Ailin showed up in the pub around noon instead of his usual late afternoon arrival. As soon as he walked in, he looked at me and said, "Come with me." Alright, finally, he's going to involve me with one of his secret operations. I was wrong. When I excitedly walked out the door with him, he said, "Let's go have some lunch at the restaurant." My excitement turned to dread as I faced the possibility of seeing Claire again. Maybe we'd have another server and not her. Could I be that lucky?

No!

As soon as we were settled she came over to our table, as plain and frumpy as ever. Her long dress hung nearly to her shoes and her hair was tied up in a knot on top of her head so tight it took the wrinkles out of her elbows. Wearing no lipstick nor makeup of any kind, she flashed a friendly smile towards Ailin. She said, "Ailin, so nice to see you. What can I bring you to drink?" She didn't ask me, nor even acknowledge my presence.

Ailin replied, "I'll have tea, Claire, and what would you like, Mark?" Again, she did not turn to face me at all.

I said, "I'll have a soda if you have one." Still without recognizing my existence, she smiled again at Ailin, turned and went back to the kitchen.

Ailin looked at me said, "What did you do to her?"

"I haven't done anything to her. I haven't spoken to her. I haven't seen her, and I certainly haven't asked her out on a date, like everyone thinks I have!"

She came back with Ailin's tea and water instead of soda for me (no ice). Hmm. We ordered lunch, at least Ailin ordered lunch. She never looked at me or asked what I wanted. She soon came back with exactly the same plates for each of us. Apparently, I was having fish & chips, just like Ailin was, whether I wanted it or not.

After our meal, she asked Ailin if he wanted some cake or pie, but he refused. And for the first time since we'd been there, she looked squarely at me and said, "I don't care who you bring in here with you, or what you're thinking, I will not go out with you and I wish you'd stop harassing me!" She then smiled at Ailin, turned, and went back into the kitchen.

Ailin said, "How many times have you asked her out?"

"I have NEVER asked her out! I think she's crazy and/or delusional."

Ailin thought a little, then said, "That's very strange, I've known Claire for a long time and she's always been very sensible and trustworthy. I'm sure you two will work out your differences."

Before I could protest further, a man I'd never seen before walked into the restaurant and Ailin waved him over. As the man neared our table, Ailin looked at me said, "Take a deep breath. It's just a bad day, not a bad life."

Ailin and the man shook hands, but didn't speak, nor did Ailin introduce him to me. Instead, he looked at the man and said, "This is Mark, the gentleman I was telling you about." The other man simply nodded. Then Ailin looked at me asked, "Mark, I'll only ask you once, and I'll never hold it against you one way or the other. But I THINK you might want to do more than you're currently doing

for me. I'm pretty sure you know what I'm talking about."
He then nodded towards his friend who then spoke for the
first time saying,

"Ailin says he trusts you, which means I trust you as well.
But I have to know something first. Are you willing to
change your life forever, to take great risks, to possibly
participate in illegal activities, all for no financial reward,
only for the love of Ireland?"

They both stared at me. Ailin then said, "It's okay to say
no; I'll totally understand. Nothing will change between
us. But if you want to join us, now is the only time we'll
ever ask."

I looked first at Ailin, then at the other man. I took a deep
breath, then another deep breath and said, "Why not? You
only live once."

Ailin nodded, but the other man replied, "FALSE. You
live every day; you only die once."

I swallowed very hard and wished I'd had something
other than warm water to drink. I then made a life
changing decision by saying, "I'm in."

With that being said, Ailin introduced us, "This is
Turlough. We'll talk later." We all shook hands and they
left me sitting in the restaurant with my head spinning.
Did I just join the IRA? At that point, I didn't really know
what I'd done, other than commit to Ailin, whom I trusted
more than any man I'd ever known before. Did I just do

something stupid? No, I'm not a stupid man! And sometimes I think that's part of the problem.

I had almost forgotten where I was as I sat there contemplating my decision-making. Suddenly, from behind me I hear, "Did you want anything else, or will that be quite enough?"

Claire, the Amite! I'll teach her a good lesson right now about who is boss here. "No ma'am, I think I'll have a piece of cake and a cup of coffee." If looks could kill, I'd be dead!

She returned about 10 minutes later and said, "Sorry, we're all out of cake."

Yeah, I'm sure you are. So I said, "Okay, I'll have a piece of pie."

As she turned to leave, her face was flushed as red as red can be, even for an Irishwoman. This time I waited about twenty minutes before she again returned empty-handed and said, "I'm so sorry, but it seems as though we're out of pie as well."

I stared into those devilish eyes and asked, "Well, what do you have?"

"All desserts are gone. The only thing we have left in the kitchen is some rhubarb casserole from yesterday."

She was not going to win! Even as I sat there and watched two other tables enjoying full meals with desserts, she was not going to win. "Okay," I said as I smiled at her,

"I'll have the rhubarb, thank you very much." Steam was venting from her ears and sparks were flying from her eyes as she wheeled her Amish self back towards the kitchen.

Twenty-five minutes later she arrived at my table and sat before me the grossest mess of disgusting matter I'd ever seen in my life, with a cup of cold coffee. Then she sweetly said, "Will there be anything else love?"

I had her now! Hearing that, I jumped up to my feet and declared for everyone in the restaurant to hear, "I knew you were in love with me. But I wouldn't marry you no matter how much you want me to be the father of your children!"

Then I triumphantly whirled away to walk out the door and tripped over a food cart. By the time I gracefully picked myself up, the man sitting next to me with his wife said, "You must really be in love with her, Sonny. Good Luck!"

12

I WAS STILL STEAMING when I entered the pub. Ruaraidh spoke to me, but I didn't pay any attention to him or what he said. He followed me to my corner table and said, "What's wrong with you?"

"Look, Ruaraidh, I have neither the time nor the crayons to explain this to you."

"Claire turned you down again didn't she? I know how she is and how mad she can make you."

"No, she most certainly did not turn me down for the simple fact that I've NEVER asked her out!"

He nodded and said, "That's not what I've heard."

"Well you heard wrong!"

He sat down across from me and very seriously asked, "Do you want my opinion on what you should do?"

"Why would I care what you think?"

He then became righteously indignant and blurted out, "By God, my opinion matters!"

"I'm sorry. Of course your opinion matters, Ruaraidh, just not to me."

Somehow, he took that as a compliment and wanted to shake my hand. Anything to get him to leave me alone. I walked outside and sat in front of the pub watching life in Dungloe pass by me. It was beautiful. Dungloe was situated between a smallish mountain range and the sea and not near any major urban areas or any major highways. The only way to get to Dungloe was to try really hard; therefore, internet coverage was spotty, or non-existent, unless you paid premium prices for it. Most people didn't. I did because I wanted to check the news from abroad. I had no email account, too dangerous, but I did check out news from America, especially the sports scores. I missed sports. Here in Ireland, it's hurling, Irish football (not like ours), and soccer. You can understand why I'm missing American sports.

But since most families can't afford the internet, kids are kids here. They ride bikes and chase dogs. Little girls make mud cakes and little boys eat them. It's like America used to be in the 1950's or 60's. I'm not sure if people lock their doors at night or not. I don't think there's a need to. I've only seen two policemen here (called Garda) and neither of them have much to do except walk around town and eat free pastries. I haven't heard of a crime being committed since I've been here. It's easy to see why people born here never want to move away.

My only complaint, so far, is the apparent lack of attractive females. Oh, there are a lot of pretty teenaged girls and some nice looking young married ladies, but the older ones have mostly gone to fat from either raising children or the Irish diet. Without a doubt, the prettiest woman of any age is Mairead, who's married to my boss and friend. The only other single woman, near my age who is not married or overweight, is the Amite, Claire. Even though I am a bit lonely for some female companionship, I'm not desperate enough yet to spend time with a plain-Jane, frumpy, ill-tempered, crazy Amish woman!

I could hardly wait for Ailin to arrive back this evening so I could start my adventures with him. No matter what he wanted me to do, it had to be better and more exciting than ordering toilet paper and signing for beer deliveries. I also wish I could stop thinking about the two million dollar life insurance policy. That just irked me to no end, knowing those two scumbags would benefit from my un-death. With three hours to go till Ailin arrived, I had too much time on my hands. I should've found something to keep me busy. I should've minded my own business. But, I didn't.

Instead, I decided to go back to my room, Google the phone number of the private detective, Desmond Jones, in Winston-Salem, and call him to see if I could find out any other information. Yeah, this is a great idea!

Figuring in the time change between here and the states, it must be early morning there and I was hoping he'd be in his office. He was. He answered, "Desmond Jones Investigations."

I said, "Is this Desmond Jones?"

"No," he said, "it's Prince Charles, or would you rather speak with the Queen?"

What?

I didn't know what to say, so following Ailin's solid advice, I said nothing. Finally, he asked, "Are you still there?"

"Yes, I'm here, but I wanted to speak with Desmond Jones, please."

"Go ahead. What do you want? I'm busy."

I said, "So, is this Desmond Jones, the private investigator?"

"Look buddy, you'd better tell me what you want right now, or I'm hanging up. I don't have time to talk to any geeches from South Carolina."

"I'm not from South Carolina, I'm calling from Ireland."

There was a moment of silence, then he said, "Well, you ain't Irish and I still think you're from South Carolina."

"I didn't say I was Irish, I said I was calling from Ireland. I want to ask you some questions about Paul Alfred."

Again, a moment of silence. Then he said, "I don't know anyone named Paul Alfred, never heard that name before."

"I know you know the name. In fact, I know you're investigating him. I just want a little information, my boss asked me to call you." It was just a little white lie.

"I don't know what you're talking about hammerhead. You and your boss can both kiss the queen's butt for all I care. Goodbye."

And he hung up on me. So, I got nowhere with that, except the reassurance that this investigator wouldn't be telling things he knew to anyone. If anyone could even stand talking to such a rude human being.

I saw Ailin come in about his usual time and motioned for the waitress to bring us over two pints. I sat down after him, prepared to sip and wait in silence until he was ready to talk. Instead, after he sat, before he sipped, he looked at me and asked, "Who told you to call Desmond Jones?" Before I could answer, he got up, left his pint on the table and walked upstairs.

At this point, not only do I not know what's going on, I wouldn't know what to do about it if I did. So here I sit, with two pints in front of me, Ailin mad and disappointed with me, and not knowing what to do about it. And

Ruaraidh walks up. "Can I bring you anything?" I didn't respond, so again, he says, "Can I bring you anything?"

"There's no need to repeat yourself, Ruaraidh. I ignored you just fine the first time." And of course, my age is very inappropriate for my behavior. It's not Ruaraidh's fault I'm stupid, but before I can apologize, he walks away.

I finish my pint in silence, then Ailin's pint as well. The music starts up and everyone seems happy and carefree. Even Ruaraidh is laughing with some friends at the bar. Little kids are dancing a jig to the music, the older people are tapping their feet to the rhythm, and teenagers are dreaming lusty thoughts of sexual conquests. Or how to sneak a pint out of the bar without their parents knowing. I sit and watch.

I silently wonder what a beautiful woman like Mairead does on these lonely nights, quite alone, sitting out near the ocean by herself. Or, is she by herself? I then wonder what a homely, frumpy Amish girl does as well. Does she just sit around tightening her bun and feeling sorry for herself? Or, is she completely content with fate's verdict for her life? My mind is so preoccupied with these thoughts that I don't notice Ruaraidh standing next to me.

He's silent as he stares at me. I say to him, "I apologize if I was rude a while ago, I didn't mean it."

He nods and tells me, "You know, Mark, now and then it's good to pause in your pursuit of happiness and just be happy."

13

I WAS NOT LOOKING forward to facing Ailin for tea and coffee, but when I arrived he was already seated and motioned for me to come over. The waitress brought me hot coffee and left without a word. He didn't waste any time saying, "Mark, you're going to have to make peace with your past so it won't screw up your future. That wasn't smart what you did yesterday. It could've gotten us both in trouble."

I didn't understand, so I asked him, "How could you get in trouble for something I did?"

He didn't hesitate, "Even though I trust this private detective in the States, what would happen if he wasn't trustworthy? What would he do if he knew of some type of reward your ex-wife or her husband were advertising for any information concerning you? When I called him, all he knew was that I was looking for information about you, as if I didn't know you. But when you called him, and trust me, he knew it was you, Mark, that opened up a ball of wax none of us wants to explore."

I never thought of these things, obviously. I told Ailin how sorry I was and I'd never do it again.

Then he continued, "Whereas he might rat you out to your ex-wife, there's still not a lot they could do to you. Whereas, if the Brits find out I've been harboring a man who is faking his own death, for whatever reason, it would be disaster for me. I'd never be able to explain it." He took a few sips of his tea before it turned cold, then said, "Mark, if you continue to work for me, I must be able to trust you and to know you're not going to do anything stupid again. Your true identity is important for us both to keep well hidden. Do you understand?"

Of course I did; I felt terrible and never realized the ramifications of my actions.

Ailin finished his tea, looked at me, and asked if everything else was good, then said, "It looks as though you probably need a haircut. Don't. Let it grow and think about a goatee as well. You've changed your name, might as well change your appearance, just to be safe. Today is the perfect day to start living your dreams. And, you never know, Claire might say 'yes' today."

And he was out the front door while I'm still sitting here thinking, "Claire?"

He was right about my hair; it hadn't been cut since I'd been here, but I'd never actually thought of letting it grow long. And I'd never even had a moustache before, let alone a goatee; however, I had learned my lesson with Ailin. If he said let it grow long, then it was going to be long.

Several weeks passed and the subject of my participation with Ailin and the IRA never came up. Of course, I said nothing. But I was ready at a moment's notice. Life was pretty routine. I was even successful at avoiding the Amite, but equally unsuccessful at talking with Mairead either. Then my luck changed for the worst one day. I had to go to the pharmacy, called a chemists over here, to get some toiletries when I ran into the Amish train from Hades.

I was completely minding my own business, trying to figure out which deodorant I should buy. I didn't recognize any of these European brands. Then I heard that voice. I turned around and without a "hello," "goodbye," or "kiss my butt," she said, "If you think I'm going to date you because you're trying to grow a goatee, like some wimpy schoolboy, you're living in a dream world! I wouldn't date you if your hair was as long as Samson's!"

Trying to hold back my temper, I said, "What's your problem? Do you hate all men, or is it just me?"

I knew that statement got to her because her face became fully flushed. Then she spouted out, "You're just like all men. I could put a blonde wig on a hot water heater and you'd try to screw it."

"Well, Missy, the hot water heater would probably have a better body than you. And definitely a better personality. And I doubt you'd know a good man if one bit you on the nose." I thought that really put her in her place.

She gritted her teeth and pursed her lips before saying, "Men! The good ones try to screw you. The bad ones do screw you. And the rest don't know how to screw you— like you!"

The chemist and several onlookers stood in total awe and silence. I didn't know what to say. Apparently the Amite had also run out of things to say. And the rest were afraid to say anything. She finally turned around and walked away. I took my few items to the chemist to pay for them and he said, "Is she really your girlfriend?"

"No, she's not my girlfriend! Who in the world would ever want to date a mean, ugly, spiteful, witch like her?"

The woman behind me then asked, "Well, why do you keep asking her out then?"

"I don't keep . . . I haven't asked . . . FORGET IT!"

I left my European deodorant and other stuff on the counter and stormed out.

Ailin struggled with calling the private detective in North Carolina again. He didn't want to raise too much suspicion, but he had to ask a few questions to ease his mind. It took several calls to eventually catch Desmond Jones at his office, but when he answered, Ailin explained his question in great detail. He wanted to know what, if any, sort of legal trouble Mark (or Paul Alfred) was in by his disappearance.

Desmond Jones was ready for that question. He'd already delved into that matter for his own curiosity. He told Ailin, "As far as I can tell, he's in no trouble at all with any legal stuff. He owed quite a few debts when he disappeared, but his wife sold all the housing properties and Walmart bought the office complex that was under construction. They paid the wife a handsome amount to get that prime piece of real estate. Then they changed the design and made it into one of their "express" stores. Not only were all the debts paid off, but she also made quite a substantial profit on the deal. So, to answer your question, he's fine legally. And his wife is even better with the sale of the properties and now, especially fine, since she's going to get a cool two million dollars from his death. He is dead isn't he, Ailin?"

Ailin, hesitated a bit, then answered, "Why would you ask such an illogical question, Desmond? He must be dead or his wife wouldn't be filing for his life insurance. Would she?"

Desmond paused, then said, "Okay, whatever you say. But tell your dead friend not to call my office anymore."

Ailin coyly replied, "Dead people don't talk, Mr. Jones. I hope you have a nice day. Please keep me posted of any new developments."

The call made Ailin feel a bit better about his friendship with Mark and eventually involving him in any activities. Up till now, he was very hesitant about using someone who might be a fugitive for any of his activities. This made things much clearer.

Fall may be the most pleasant time of year in Ireland. There seems to be a respite from the summertime rains and winter storms. Cool, crisp days, mostly sunny, with temperate evenings improved everyone's mood, with the exception of a certain Amite. Fall also meant the official end of "tourist season" in most of Ireland. Dungloe, of course, didn't have to worry with that. But people in the other regions, especially in the south and west, were happy to have their country to themselves again. Without having to answer the same four questions a hundred times a day from each and every tourist they met:

Does it rain all the time here?

Is there a McDonald's in town?

Why do you drive on the wrong side of the road? And,

How far is Dublin from here?

I know the Irish love their capital city, Dublin, but it does irritate those in the rest of the country that tourists think Ireland begins with Dublin and ends with kissing the Blarney Stone. Once, when I was complaining to Ailin about the lack of attractive, available women in town, I mentioned I might go to Dublin one weekend just to experience some Irish women. He looked at me and said, "If all the women in Dublin were laid end to end, I wouldn't be surprised."

It took me a few moments to understand that.

14

AILIN WAS UNUSUALLY quiet for the next few weeks. We'd meet each morning and evening, but other than listen to my rundown of the day's events, he was quite subdued. I didn't know what this meant, but I did know not to ask anything. I had a suspicion it was about Mairead. I knew he still loved her with all his heart and it was extremely hard for him to be apart from her.

One evening, during a long period of silence, I asked him to help me understand the situation with Northern Ireland and the British. Like most people, I knew a little, but certainly not everything. This seemed to perk him up a bit. "How deeply do you want me to go Mark?"

"Deep enough so that I'll understand why you're so passionate about it." I answered.

He took a long drink of Guinness then asked me, "How would you feel if your neighbor, Canada, came and annexed 6 of your states without any reason and wouldn't give them back?"

I thoughtfully replied, "Well, I've been to Canada and I've always gotten the impression that I could take that country over in about two days." He was not amused at my attempt at levity.

After a suitable period of ensuring I regretted my last statement, he said, "Mark, a man has to stand up for what is right, even if he's standing alone. Our lives begin to end the day we become silent about things that matter."

He then spent roughly forty-five minutes giving me the history of Northern Ireland, Britain, and the Republic of Ireland. That was entirely more than I wanted to hear or could understand, but I listened. In a nutshell, years ago Britain "owned" all of Ireland, but after a bloody revolution Ireland was granted its independence from Britain in 1921, all but six counties in the north. The other twenty-six counties became the Republic of Ireland and the northern six stayed with Britain. This had been the boiling point ever since. There were some religious issues and lots of other "stuff," but the bottom line was that Britain owned the six counties and the IRA wanted them back.

Ailin also explained to me a bit of his part, saying, "We know there's nothing we can do to change the British government and force them to give us back our land; however, we can make them regret they're here and make their existence as uncomfortable as possible. All this in the hopes that the cumulative effects of all our 'shenanigans' may entice them to leave our country of their own accord. However, I'm convinced of one thing, Mark, what's meant to be will always find a way."

I had also been very successful at avoiding the A-Train, Claire. I'd only seen her once, when Ailin insisted I join him for lunch one day. By some miracle we had a different young lady as our server. She was plain, pleasant, and pregnant, and I could barely understand a word she said. Ailin explained she was Gaelic, from the northern section of Donegal, and that she had married a local boy. They lived in the country where he herded sheep and fished some as the need arose.

I didn't understand the phrase, ". . . as the need arose." What did that mean? When they were hungry, he fished? Fortunately, Ailin sensed my futility and continued, "He goes out on the big fishing boats, the kind that are gone anywhere from three to six months at a time. No one enjoys that sort of life, but it pays extremely well and affords people to do other things they do enjoy, like herding sheep and supporting their family."

"Trust me," he continued, "it's a young man's job. There are very few people who can put up with being gone up to six months at a time, rolling about in the Atlantic, with virtually no assurance that you'll even return."

This fascinated me. So I asked, "It's all young guys trying to make some money, then?"

"Yes," he answered, "except the old guys who own the boats and make the 'big money.' The old fishermen will never stop or never die, they just smell that way."

"Did you ever go out on the boats, Ailin?"

"Only once." he replied, "After my last year in school I needed some money and took a job as a 'helper' on one of the trawlers. In those days we were out only several weeks at a time, not months. I was seasick the first week, then I was weak and sick from throwing up so much that I had to stay in bed the next week. When we finally came back to port, the old captain only paid me for three days work, saying 'I'm not paying anybody to stay in bed and sleep. Here, take this, be glad you're getting anything. And don't come back.' I didn't."

I was so enthralled with the story I never noticed the Amite standing behind me. When Ailin finished speaking, she said, "Was everything alright with the food and your service, Ailin?"

"Yes, Claire, it was grand. Your new girl did a fantastic job, I think she'll work out fine."

I was holding my breath, waiting for the onslaught, but she simply said, "Thanks," and walked away.

Whew . . . I could exhale. We went outside and Ailin's friend Turlough was waiting for him.

He started to walk away and said, "I'll see you later tonight and, oh, it looks like you and Claire have made up. Good job!"

Made up? Are you kidding me? I've never asked her out. I don't want to ask her out. I've never been turned down, because I've never asked her out, and now I've made up with her? Next thing I know, I'll be having babies with her without ever having sex with her Amish self. Not that I would want to.

One of the mysteries I haven't solved yet is why Mairead only shows up in the pub on nights when Ailin isn't here—like tonight. I don't know where he is, or when he'll be back, but she's here, and as beautiful as ever. I was sitting at the end of the bar listening to the music, as usual. Tonight was really a treat because a little kid, probably not more than 7 or 8 years old, was playing fiddle. I hadn't seen him before, but the regulars all seemed to know him.

The regular players started, again without any music or without any discussion between them. They just started playing. The little boy, whose name I can't pronounce, but its spelled Conlaoth, waited a few minutes, and without any urging, coaxing or persuading that I could see, commenced.

Magic is the only word I know to describe what Conlaoth did. There is no other way to illustrate or portray what happened next. Everyone sat spellbound, except for the other players, who rightfully deferred to this genius. I thought for sure the strings would catch fire he was moving the bow so quickly across them. I don't know how long this lasted; time either stood still or expanded, I don't know which. But suddenly all the other players stopped, and for a quick second, Conlaoth did as well. Then he changed gears completely and started playing the most beautiful, symphonic, operatic melody you've ever heard in your life. I don't know if it was Beethoven, Mozart, or something he made up. All I know is that EVERYONE in the pub was spellbound.

When he completed his magical spell, the room burst into applause and Conlaoth ran to his parents arms, apparently a little embarrassed and bashful. After a few minutes, he and his parents left the pub and the regulars started up again. I motioned for Ruaraidh to bring me another pint, which he was always happy to do. He was never the sort of bartender to ever ask if you think you'd had enough. When he came over, I said, "That was absolutely amazing!"

"What?"

"The little boy playing that fiddle, or violin or whatever it was."

He sort of nodded and said, "Everybody has talents. We can all do something."

"Really? Tell me what you can do, Ruaraidh."

He became a bit indignant and quickly said, "Well I may not be that funny or athletic, or good-looking, or smart, or talented . . . I forgot where I was going with this." And he quickly walked away.

It was then I looked across the room and saw Mairead sitting quite alone and motioning for me to join her. She was a vision. A Da Vinci in a world of caricaturists. Any description I can give of her would be totally inadequate and insufficient to do her justice. Unlike most Irish women, she has dark, flowing hair and luminescent blue eyes. She has a woman's body— not a teenager's, not a runway model's, but a woman's body. Her legs are long and shapely with perfectly contoured ankles, calves, and knees. Her smile is intoxicating and her face was sculpted by Michelangelo. And, she is married to my boss, my friend, and probably the best man I've ever known.

15

I WALKED OVER to Mairead's table and sat across from her, and when she smiled at me I nearly fainted. She said, "That was extraordinary, don't you think? Or, do you see that type of thing regularly in America?"

I answered, "I don't think you can see that kind of talent anywhere, especially from an eight year old." We made small talk about the weather, small town living, my duties, but nothing about Ailin. I would never broach that subject with her, mainly because I wouldn't know how. Also, it's still none of my business.

We played a little game between us, in between sips of my Guinness and her glass of red wine. Every time someone walked past us, she would ask me to tell her what I THOUGHT that person would be like. Then she would correct me and tell how they really were. For instance, a heavy man with a limp walked past and I guessed he was an ex-fisherman who injured his leg on the boat and was now a potato farmer. She corrected me and said, "No, he's actually the loan officer at the bank here in town. You should be nice to him."

On and on we went with this game. I never came close to actually guessing what, or who, anyone was. My last guess was a young lady about nineteen or twenty I would imagine. She was trying her best to look and walk as sexy as possible. I looked at Mairead and said, "This young lady was probably the high school beauty queen who now works in a beauty shop cutting other women's hair."

Mairead said nothing, which was odd. So, I also said nothing further. The young lady came back past our table carrying two pints of some light-colored beer and stopped, saying to Mairead, "Good evening ma'am. You're out sort of late aren't you?"

Uh oh! This was not what I was expecting. Mairead smiled, looked over the young lady from head to toe and said, "Deidre, my dear, there's a fine line between 'sultry' and 'slutty.' Find it." Of course, Deidre had no response to that and quickly walked away.

After a moment or two, I said, "Well that was interesting."

Mairead smiled and replied, "She's the daughter of the richest man in town. Not the nicest man by any means, but the richest—next to Ailin, of course." Then she became quiet, which meant I also became quiet. She slowly sipped her wine and we both listened to the music.

When Mairead finished her glass of wine, she completely surprised me and asked if I'd like to go outside and sit at a table where it wasn't so noisy. I took my drink with me, she didn't want another glass of wine, or anything— she wanted to talk. She started, "I guess Ailin has told you about our situation and our history, so I guess it's important I should tell you the truth. Which may or may not be Ailin's version. Probably not, since it will actually be the truth.

Without any response from me, she started with, "Being Irish, Ailin has always had an abiding sense of tragedy, which has sustained him through temporary periods of joy. I guess this is why all his books are so popular. It's even what attracted me to him initially. But it grows tiresome eventually. Don't get me wrong, Mark. Should I continue to call you Mark?"

"Sure, it makes it easier for everyone."

"I still love Ailin, I guess I always will. He's a good man, an honest man, very trustworthy and very idealistic. Very serious. All the time. ALL the time." I've already decided that my nodding every now and then is the best response I can have. "Whether or not his story of the British drugging him and planting the girl and manufacturing the video is true or not, is still not the real issue. The most important thing to me is that he first denied any of it happened. Then he tried to downplay it, not knowing I'd already seen the video. When I asked him specific questions, he lied to me. Having seen the video, I knew exactly what happened."

"But he continued lying to me. Then, instead of apologizing for the whole mess, he tried to blame the British for everything, which he is still doing to this day. Maybe the British planned it, maybe they were behind it all. Maybe not. Perhaps they did prey on him and he fell into their trap; however, they didn't force him to lie to me. They haven't made him not apologize to me, and they certainly haven't coerced him not to take some sort of personal responsibility for his actions. All I ever wanted him to say was, 'I made a huge mistake. I'm terribly sorry. Please forgive me.' But he never has. In his mind, it's all the fault of the British and he's blameless. And you know what, Mark, I'm not totally convinced the British had anything to do with it."

I have no idea what to say or how to react. Fortunately for me, she continued talking. "Mark, I know you have this preconception about Ailin. But, listen to me, God is fully aware that you and I are not perfect. And let me add, God is also fully aware that the people you think are perfect, are not. Like Ailin. I'm asking you to be careful who you trust. The devil was once an angel."

I had to change the subject quickly. She was telling me way more than I wanted to hear. So I said, "Tell me a little about this rich man, the girl in the pub's father.

"Sure." And it seemed as though her whole demeanor changed. "His family has always had money and a lot of land. He was privileged and, truth be known, bought his way through university. He also bought his position as head of public schools in our district, which he now runs like he's a Nazi. He's the imbecile who started the program of giving all 'participants' in football, and all sports, a trophy for participating. Not just the winners, but every little kid gets one. It's crazy. He then organized the movement not to hold back any child who failed their grades. He didn't want to 'hurt anyone's feelings.' Now, the kids know they don't have to study hard, because they're going to get passed along anyway.

"This whole political correctness thing is insane! Some people win and some lose. That's life! Some kids do well and succeed; others do not. But, we as a society, cannot continue this policy of inclusivity. Before long we'll end up like Denmark or, God forbid, Sweden!"

Unknowingly, I have really opened up a can of worms. Then she calmed down a little bit and said, "And worst of all, when Ailin and I first separated, he hit on me continually for weeks on end."

"What did you do?" I asked.

"The last time, when he cornered me in a hallway at the pub, and asked if I was 'interested in a good time,' I'd had enough of him, so I grabbed his crotch rather firmly and said, 'If you weren't hung like a hamster, I might consider it.' He hasn't bothered me since. He only confirmed what my mother always told me—the worst thing about some men is that when they're not drunk, they're sober."

We sat in silence for a few moments, then she said, "You can obviously not answer this question, but I'm going to ask anyway. You don't have to explain anything to me, but I'm curious, are you married or not?"

"No, I'm not married. I'm quite divorced and glad of it."

"Does that mean you don't want to marry again?"

"Not at all. I'm just glad I'm not married to my ex-wife any longer. She wasn't who I thought she was, and she was definitely not a good person."

Mairead smiled a little, the sort of smile that could drive men crazy. Then said, "All men like to think they are marrying nymphomaniacs. The problem is, after a few years, the nympho leaves and the maniac stays."

She rose from the table and said, "I'd better be going home. Good luck explaining our 'conversation' to Ailin tomorrow."

A little nervously, I replied, "What do you mean?"

She simply smiled again and walked towards her car. And trust me on this—she knows how to walk.

I was a little apprehensive with Ailin in the morning over our coffee and tea, but the conversation was the usual daily activities and plans. Then something different happened. He asked, "Can you be free this afternoon?"

"Of course I can. What do you want me to do?"

He nodded and said, "I'll pick you up about half one." He took the last sip of his tea and started for the door, then stopped, turned around and asked, "How was your date with Mairead last night?"

Before I could answer, he turned back around and kept on walking out the door. How did he know? And what makes him think it was a date? I've got to set this straight as soon as I see him again.

At 1:30 a car pulled up in front of the pub with Turlough driving. No one else was inside. I got in and asked no questions and he didn't volunteer anything. After about 10 minutes, he looked over at me and said, "Mairead? Really? I thought you were dating Claire!"

"I'm not dating anybody! Certainly not Mairead, or that Amish witch!"

He frowned a bit and said, "She's not Amish. Why would you think that?"

"Look Turlough, I'm not dating either one of them. I never have and never will. Mairead is Ailin's wife. Why would anyone think I was dating her?"

He must've taken his lessons from Ailin because he became silent as well. We rode in total awkwardness for close to an hour, until he pulled into a driveway leading to an old stone farmhouse that had no roof. There was shrubbery and overgrown weeds all around it and growing inside it. Ailin and two other men were also inside waiting.

We walked in and Ailin introduced everyone to me, but I couldn't understand what their names were. No one else but Ailin spoke. He asked the others if everything was set up. They all said 'yes' then they all looked at me and

Ailin said, "Are you ready to help?" I said yes, even though I had no idea what sort of help I'd be giving.

16

TURLOUGH AND I got in our car and the others left in two cars that were hidden behind the farm house. I really had no idea where we were or where we were going, but I saw signs for Londonderry, which I knew was in Northern Ireland. Just before the border, we pulled off into a gas station that had closed. Ailin was waiting for us with the others.

Ailin motioned for me to come over to his car, which I did, while the others remained where they were. When I walked up to the car, I tried to open the passenger side door, but couldn't because it was locked. I looked in and the front seat and floor boards were covered with all sorts of electronic equipment. Ailin told me to get in the back seat, which I did. I'd already made my mind up I wasn't doing anything else until I set the record straight about my so-called date with Mairead last night.

Before he could speak I said, "Ailin, I want you to know that I was only at the pub last night by myself and Mairead asked me to sit and talk with her. That's all. It wasn't a date. It wasn't planned and all we did was talk for a few minutes."

He looked at me from the rearview mirror and replied, "I know that. I just wanted to see what YOU thought it was. I won't ask you what you talked about, first because I don't want you to lie to me. And second, it's none of my business. Everything is cool, Mark. Now, here's what I need you to do."

He didn't tell me everything; in fact, he told me virtually nothing. I'm guessing he figured the less I knew, the better off we both were. Basically, my job was to drive Ailin's car, the one with all the electronic equipment in it, and monitor any communications. Apparently, this equipment was somehow tuned in to the British police networks and could listen in to all radio calls between officers and the police headquarters.

Ailin wanted me to monitor the network and listen to all the communications. He then gave me the address and name of a British government building where they were going to sneak in. It was some sort of holiday in Britain and all government offices were closed. If I heard the address or name of the building come across any of the radio networks, I was to call Ailin immediately on a walkie talkie he gave me, and tell them to leave the building.

He didn't tell me why they were breaking into the building, what they'd be doing, or how long the entire operation would take. I was to just sit there, monitor the radio, and let them know if I heard anything about the address. When we arrived at the building, they all got out and disappeared around the corner. I must tell you, I was very nervous.

If caught, certainly, they'd find my true identity and probably either put me in jail, deport me, or maybe shoot me, depending on what type of illegal activity Ailin and the boys were up to. Fortunately, it was raining lightly and there weren't a lot of people on the streets of Londonderry. An old woman passed by and stared at me sitting in the car. I waved to her, then thought, "That was pretty stupid. Crooks don't wave to people."

Then a little boy came around the corner riding a bicycle and stopped beside my car. I rolled down the window to see what he wanted and he asked me if I'd seen a black dog come by here. "No," I said and he was off. I was sweating bullets. I was simply hoping we'd make our getaway unscathed at this point. I heard nothing of any consequence on the radio equipment and had no reason to call Ailin, except I wanted to tell them to hurry up!

After about twenty-five minutes, they came walking around the corner, quite casually, drinking tea and carrying bags of food. Ailin asked if I wanted fish and chips or brown bread. I was much too nervous to eat or drink anything. I just wanted to leave and get out of Londonderry and Northern Ireland—back to my safe little pub in Dungloe.

I got back in the car with Turlough, Ailin drove his car and the other two lads took off in their car. We all went in different directions as casually and easily as you please.

No police sirens, no chases, no excitement. If I hadn't been scared to death, this whole IRA thing would have been quite boring!

Turlough obviously wasn't going to say anything, so finally I did. "What did you guys do back there?"

"Best you don't know, mate."

"Well, since I'm now involved in it, I think I have the right to know!"

Turlough looked over and replied, "We simply made a deposit and a withdrawal."

"What? That wasn't a bank. That makes no sense at all."

He grinned and said, "I am under no obligation to make sense to you." And he said no more all the way back to Dungloe.

Turlough dropped me off at the pub and drove away. I didn't see Ailin or the others anywhere, I have no idea where they went. I walked in, finally relieved of tension, and Ruaraidh yells at me, "Claire is looking for you. Where have you been?"

"Why is she looking for me? Is something wrong?"

"How would I know? She's your girlfriend."

Ruaraidh just snickered after saying that, making sure everyone in the pub could hear it as well. I thought of some mean things to reply with, but I kept quiet. I wanted to say something ill and dirty. But I didn't. Instead I was wondering and dreading what in the world the Amite witch could want from me.

I walked down to the restaurant and looked in the front window. Everything seemed fine. People were eating and the staff was operating. I started not to go in, then she came from the back and saw me. I didn't have to go in because she rushed out the door to accost me outside on the street.

"Where the devil have you been? The only time we ever need you and you disappear. You just wait till I tell Ailin about this!"

"Well, Missy," I said, feeling quite confident of myself, "I've been with Ailin all afternoon. If you still want to call him, just go right ahead."

She was fuming! She started to turn around, then looked at me and said, "If I throw a stick, will you leave?"

That was it! I got up in her face and screamed, "I don't know what your problem is woman, but I bet it's hard to pronounce!"

Everyone on the street and in the restaurant was looking at us now. She said, very slowly, "No, in fact, it's very easy. My problem is pronounced MARK!"

❧

The day's activities had me so pumped up that I could barely sit still. I was hoping Ailin would come in the pub this evening so we could discuss our great adventure. But he didn't show up. Neither did Mairead and I was left to my own thoughts and Ruaraidh. He didn't ask, but he was definitely curious as to my whereabouts this afternoon.

Still being excited, I probably drank a little more than I should have. I even had a fairly intelligent conversation with Ruaraidh so I knew I had been drinking too much. He kept beating around the bush, trying to find out where I had been and what I did this afternoon. I should've kept my mouth shut, or walked away, but I didn't. I was a little proud of my part in whatever it was we did today. I knew I could not discuss it with anyone, especially Ruaraidh, but the Guinness dulled my senses a bit and our foray into Londonderry was still fresh on my mind. So, I asked him a question about what he thought of the situation with Northern Ireland and how he felt about that country.

He took a small sip of some amber-colored drink and quite thoughtfully replied, "You can't be a real country unless you have a beer and an airline like us. It helps if you have some kind of football team or some nuclear weapons. But at the very least you need a beer. And all they have is a lousy football team. So, in my opinion, they're not a country. They're not really Irish, and they're certainly not British. In my opinion, they're screwed!"

I'm sitting here trying to digest Ruaraidh's comments and I want to laugh them off, but somehow, they're making sense to me. Is it the Guinness? Or has he actually made a sensible statement? The more I think about it, the more confused I'm making myself. Sometimes, it isn't what you don't know that gets you into trouble; it's what you know for sure that just isn't so.

I decided to give up and go home. I told Ruaraidh I was leaving because I was feeling a bit drunk. He said, "You're okay. You're not drunk if you can lie on the floor without holding on." For the second time this evening, he made sense to me; therefore, I knew for sure I had to go home and sleep it off.

17

THE NEXT SEVERAL WEEKS were fairly uneventful. I had no further involvements with Ailin and his boys, but I'm certain they were doing things. Obviously, they didn't need my help with anything. I was even successful at avoiding the Amite and her despicable and contemptible personality. The only time I had to go in the restaurant she was not there, and I was very grateful for that.

One Saturday, my off day, I decided to take the bus back over to the neighboring, little, fishing village of Burtonport. I wanted to explore the scenic village with the winding streets and coastal views. Burtonport had several cottages with thatched roofs, which really fascinated me. It was also located on a small bluff, or cliff, which afforded it a grand view of the ocean. I'm not sure why the tourist industry hasn't promoted Burtonport more. Maybe because it's so small, or hard to get to. I'm not sure.

I walked around town a few minutes (that's really all it took) and ended up back in the pub I'd visited the first time I was here. It wasn't raining, but it wanted to. Most of the people I saw were scurrying about doing their shopping and errands before the rain started. It wasn't warm, but a light jacket was all I needed to be comfortable. Taking Ailin's advice, I'd let my hair grow and was quite proud of it now. I kept it tied in back most of the time; it was easier that way than to let it be loose. My goatee, in contrast, had not completely filled in. I guess I was lucky in that my beard didn't grow very fast. But it frustrated me a bit because it continued to look so scraggly.

I had a bowl of the homemade soup, again delicious, but hard to tell what was in it. There was a high cliff outside of town that looked interesting and I wanted to go up there to see what the view was like. I didn't know how far it was, or even if there was a road up there, but I didn't want to walk it. I really should start exercising a bit . . . but not today. I remember what Ruaraidh told me when I first arrived and I asked him if there was a good place to exercise in town. He cocked his head a little, as though I was speaking a foreign language and then said, "Exercise? Exercise might make you feel better and look better naked. But so does tequila."

So, I looked around to see if there was a taxi in town. Around the corner, parked outside a small grocery store, was a non-descript vehicle with someone sitting inside. There was a sign post next to it that said, "For Hire." I walked up to the driver's side and the window rolled down. What seemed to be a very attractive woman, who was working a crossword puzzle, said to me, "Can I help you?"

I asked her if this was a taxi. She replied, "That depends."

I nodded and said, "Depends on what?"

She put the crossword down on the seat, looked back up at me saying, "First, do you have any money? Second, where do you want to go? And, third, who are you? I've never seen you before?"

I really didn't think I owed her any explanations, but what was the harm? It was her car and her town, and she was very pretty.

I answered, "Yes, I have SOME money. Not a lot, in case you were thinking of robbing me. Second, I want to go up there." I was pointing up to the high cliff. "And, third, I'm not from around here."

She looked at me and replied, "American?"

Obviously, my North Carolina accent wasn't fooling anyone. "Yes. Can you take me up to the cliff?"

She sat thinking for a moment while I realized exactly how pretty she was. She finally said, "You're not going to jump off are you?"

"No, I just wanted to see what the view was like up there. I bet it's nice."

"It is. Hop in. Cost you four Euro to go up there and back, or I can just drop you off up there for two Euro."

"No. Up there and back is great, thanks."

It took about four or five minutes to make the drive up the steep slope, finally arriving at an open grassy area, with no benches, fences, or anything else—but wind. Initially, I hadn't realized how hard the wind was blowing until I tried to open the car door. Pushing and straining on that door was probably more exercise than I'd had since I arrived. When I finally got out of the car, the wind was blowing so hard that it whipped my hair until the little rubber band I'd been using to tie my hair back with was blown off and away before I knew what had happened.

My longish hair was now whipping all over my face and it was very uncomfortable. I started to get back in the car for some relief when I noticed the driver had opened her door and was coming around the front of the car. She said, "Turn around!" I turned facing the wind, which was now blowing my hair away from my face.

She stood facing me and pulled something out of her coat pocket and said, "Be still." She reached up and pulled my hair together at the back of my head and tied it with something that I couldn't see. As she was doing this, her face was about four inches from mine. And even though the wind was blowing 40 miles per hour, she smelled as wonderful and sweet and sexy as any woman I'd ever been around.

As she finished tying my hair, I looked into those green eyes, and before she could back away, I kissed her. I hadn't planned on kissing her. I knew nothing about her. I didn't know if she was married or not. I didn't know if she had a gun and would shoot me. I didn't even know her name. But I kissed her. And, she kissed me back!

Time is such a relative matter. If you're walking across hot, burning coals, five seconds seems like an hour. But if you're kissing a pretty girl, an hour seems like five seconds. I don't know how long we kissed, but when we stopped, if she had punched me in the nose, it would've been worth it. But she didn't. Instead, she smiled and said, "You'll still have to pay me the four Euros."

She said, "Follow me." At that point in time, I'd have followed her off the cliff— maybe. Instead, we went back to the side of the car away from the wind and sat on the ground, leaning against the car. The view from this side was less dramatic, but it was out of the full force of the wind. She said, "This is why no one comes up here. The wind blows hard all the time. It comes from America, across the North Atlantic, with nothing to hinder it until it hits us in the face."

Okay Mark, or Paul, or whatever I'm calling myself today, what just happened? I kissed a pretty girl. On further inspection, I kissed a beautiful woman. Green eyes framed by light brown hair, with a slight tinge of red it seems. High cheek bones, full lips, small breasts, I think, but it's hard to be sure because of her jacket. Not tall, like Mairead, but not short either. And not fat, which is a little unusual for a woman her age here in Ireland. I'm totally guessing she might be about thirty, certainly not older than thirty-three.

Neither of us has spoken since we sat down out of the wind. We're sitting close, but not actually touching each other, and not daring to look at each other either. Finally, I get up the nerve and ask, "What's your name?" As I turned to look at her for her response, she leaned over and kissed me again. This kiss was not as long as the one before, but better.

She quickly said, "I'm sorry, I didn't mean to do that. I don't know what came over me." She looked back towards the ocean and said, "My name is Niamh. It's the name of the daughter of the Sea God, Manannan, a beautiful princess who rides a white horse. She comes from Tir-na-nOg, 'The Land of the Young,' which is a supernatural realm of everlasting youth, beauty, health, abundance, and joy, where three hundred years passed in what seemed like three weeks."

Without her asking me, and feeling quite full of myself, I said, "My name's Mark. I come from the Northlands of Carolina, from the tribe of Tarheels, and have ventured across the wild Atlantic in search of a princess who has lost her way for the past three hundred years."

Hoping this didn't offend her too much, I looked over and she kissed me again. Longer this time. After this kiss, we both sat back and stared at the ocean for a few moments, until she said, "And how long do you think Mark will keep up his search for the elusive princess?"

"Until the princess finds her way out of the darkness and realizes the beauty within her and without her." I didn't know what this meant, but I remembered the phrase from an old Beatles' tune, and it seemed to fit the occasion.

She hesitated for a few seconds and then replied, "Then you may find peace of mind is waiting there. And the time will come when you see we're all one."

DID SHE JUST QUOTE BEATLES' LYRICS? Quickly I'm trying to hum the tune in my mind and sing the verses in my head. But I can't remember them all, it was, at best, an obscure song. No one can know those lyrics!

Then her cell phone rang. She looked at it, then looked at me, and said, "I have to take this." She answered the call and said, "Hello . . . okay, okay. Yes. I'll be there. Bye."

And she told me we had to go. Dang! Dang! Double Dang!! We drove back into town in silence and she stopped at the pub. I fished out four Euro from my pocket to pay her, wondering what else to do or say.

She said, "I'm sorry, I have an emergency. Too bad you're from America and not from Burtonport. Thank you for a lovely afternoon, but I really have to go."

I got out of the car, holding the four Euro and still not knowing what to say. I closed the door and she looked at me with those emerald eyes and all I could think to say was, "Maybe I'll move to Burtonport." She smiled and drove away.

18

I RODE THE BUS BACK to Dungloe. I'm sure of this because I arrived back in town; however, I don't remember anything of the ten mile trip. My mind was on the cliff experience with Niamh. Niamh, Niamh, Niamh . . . I can't stop thinking about her. After the phone call she received, things happened so quickly I didn't have time to think. I should've asked what her last name was. I should've asked for her phone number. I should've asked her to run away with me to the land of Tir-na-nOg, or at least to Penny Lane. But I did none of these. Now I'm wondering and hoping and praying that she'll remember me until I can get back to Burtonport again and find her.

I left the bus and walked down the street to the pub to have a sandwich and a drink. It had started raining again and, with the change in seasons, was dark much earlier now. Back in America, this would be a time for non-stop advertising for Halloween and Thanksgiving. Probably Christmas as well. But I'm assuming they don't do Halloween here, or Thanksgiving, since I haven't heard either of them mentioned by anyone. And, thinking about that, why would they celebrate Thanksgiving here? I'm sure most Irishmen could care less about the Pilgrims.

One thing that would never change, however, was my friend Ruaraidh. He would always be there, behind the bar, serving drinks, drinking drinks, and talking about drinks. Always ready to comfort me with a few kind words. I walked around to the end of the bar and he came over, looked at me, and said, "Are you gay?"

"What in the world are you talking about?

"Well, why do you have a pink hair clip in your hair?"

I reached back to touch my hair and felt something tying my hair back. Oh, yes, Niamh tied my hair with something up on the cliff. I pulled the clip out and looked at it— a pink clip with little hearts all over it.

Ruaraidh, still standing there watching, said, "I'm not judging, but now it's easier to understand why you're not banging Claire."

"I didn't . . . what? Banging Claire? Are you crazy?"

He said, "A man's gotta do what a man's gotta do." He walked to the other end of the bar, pointing back at me as he spoke to some old drunks. Let him think what he wants, I've got the hair clip! I have something of Niamh's to hold on to. To touch, to feel, to dream about— I'm happy.

Monday morning, Ailin was drinking his tea when I arrived. I sat and the waitress brought my coffee. He sipped. And I sipped. I waited, but he just kept sipping his tea. Eventually, he looked up and said, "I don't judge men, and no one's personal lifestyle will affect their relationship with me."

It took me about ten seconds to realize he was referring to me. That crazy Ruaraidh! I explained the entire hair clip story to him and even my meeting with Niamh. He grinned and replied, "Don't worry what Ruaraidh thinks; he doesn't do it very often." He asked several questions about Niamh, none of which I had answers for. I knew virtually nothing about her, except the dream I have.

Ailin nodded thoughtfully and said, "It's the possibility of having a dream come true that makes life interesting."

We both had second cups and enjoyed the silence of each other's company. As he was rising to leave, he looked down and said, "We might need you again soon. Do you still want to help?"

"Of course I do. Anytime, just let me know." He nodded and was off again doing whatever it is he does all day to thwart the British and reunite his country. Or not; I truly have no idea what he does. I made my usual rounds, checking all the businesses, except the restaurant. I'm sure things are fine there. I did some ordering, checked invoices, monitored inventory and supplies, and answered questions. Most everyone was getting used to me and was comfortable with me now. I was beginning not to be the "new guy" anymore. Increasingly, I was just plain old Mark, or, the American.

As I was checking some invoices, the phone rang. It was the new girl at the restaurant who told me Claire needed to see me at once. Oh, great! But first, I had to check to make sure all the pictures were hung straight. Then I needed to ensure all my pencils were sharpened and that the restrooms had enough toilet paper. Finally, as I was looking at the local paper to see who won last night's game between Letterkenny and Ballyliffin, the phone rang again.

Even though our phone doesn't have caller ID, I knew who it was. And I knew she was steaming on the other end. But before I could get down to the restaurant, I still had to make sure Ruaraidh had enough clean glasses in the pub. We NEED clean glasses.

Okay, let's get it over with. The restaurant was packed and everyone was quite busy, even the witch from Hades. I stood around the cash register waiting for her until she had a moment. She walked over and contemptuously remarked "You're not allowed in that cash register, only Ailin and I can open it up." Take a deep breath, Mark. Count to ten, Paul. But no, she kept on, "Where have you been? I called for you half an hour ago!"

"Well, if you were actually my boss, I might've stopped reading the paper and come right over. But since you're not . . ."

It was all she could do not to start screaming at me. She gritted her teeth and said, "I seldom need anything from you, but when I call, it's important."

"I know."

She pursed her lips and spat out, "Any fool can know. The point is to understand."

"Oh, I understand alright," I said as I gazed into those evil eyes, "I understand that YOU need ME!"

I actually saw a twitch near her left eye as she replied, "Some people are so dumb they have to be watered twice a week. Come with me!" And she turned and walked her Amish, she-devil self back towards the kitchen. She went into a small room and came out with a piece of paper and handed it to me saying, "This is my vacation schedule. Make sure Ailin gets it and lines up a replacement."

I knew I had her going now and I couldn't let up. "Oh, I'll take care of it," I said, "and I'm sure it won't be too difficult to replace you."

Daggers were flying out of her eyes directly into my heart. I followed her out of the kitchen, back into the restaurant, feeling really proud of myself. And just as I was nearing the door, she said, in a loud voice that everyone in the restaurant could hear, "I'm sorry I've broken your heart and that you stay up all night crying, but I WILL NOT DATE YOU! Please get that through your thick skull. Now leave me alone!" She returned to the kitchen as everyone in the restaurant stopped eating and drinking and started staring at me. That dang Amite!

Each evening I sat and discussed everything important and trivial with Ailin. But no invitation to join him on any excursions came. He didn't discuss those activities and he never discussed Mairead. He did ask me about Niamh. But since I didn't know her last name, or how to contact her, or for that matter, even if I'd ever see her again, I had no information to volunteer. He nodded and said, "I'm sorry, but remember this: it's never too late to live happily ever after."

Feeling sorry for myself, I replied, "Maybe I'm getting too old to find that magic. I'm not twenty years old anymore."

He set his pint down rather firmly, lowered his head and said, "You are not too old, and it is not too late! It's up to YOU to see the beauty of everyday things. Today can be the beginning of anything you want."

19

I WAS LOOKING FORWARD to Saturday when I could take the bus back over to Burtonport and head directly to the taxi stand again . . . until I got a phone call Friday morning from Mairead. She said, "Mark, I need to talk to you as soon as I can. It's important. I'm out of town today, but I'll be back tomorrow. Can you come by my house then?"

My mind was saying, "No, I've got to go to Burtonport and see if I can find this elusive woman." But my mouth said, "Sure, I'll be there whenever you want me to."

She thanked me and asked if I could be there about 10:00. And then she said, "And don't eat breakfast, I'll whip up something for us."

"Whip up something for us??" When a beautiful woman says she'll "whip up something," your mind goes in a thousand different directions. Then, you stop and think: Ailin, friend, boss, wife. Dang, life is hard. Not really because I'm doing anything wrong, just because it's hard.

My latest dilemma: Do I tell Ailin that I'm going to his wife's house when I meet him tonight? I will not lie to him again. Fortunately, he didn't show up this evening. I listened to music for a bit and talked with Ruaraidh and some of the regulars. I was sitting there quite content in my thoughts of emerald eyes and the certain daughter of a Sea God when I heard a disturbance at the bar. I looked over and Ruaraidh was yelling at an older guy named Aengus, who was pointing his finger and jabbing Ruaraidh in the chest.

When they saw me walking over, Aengus turned away saying a few Gaelic words to Ruaraidh, which I obviously didn't understand, but knew full well what they meant. I asked Ruaraidh what happened, and said, "Ah, it was nothing."

"It looked like he was pretty mad at you to be nothing."

Ruaraidh took a long drink of beer then said, "Everyone appreciates your honesty, until you're honest with them, then you're a butthole."

"What did you tell him?"

"He asked me if I thought Muirren would go out on a date with him."

I knew Muirren. She was a nice older lady who'd been single for several years. I continued, "What did you say to him?"

Ruaraidh replied, "I told him, 'no, I don't think she will.'"

"And I'm guessing he didn't like that answer."

"Well, he asked me why I thought she'd say 'no', and I told him because he was old, dirty, and smelled like rotten fish. That was what he didn't like."

I'd not spoken to Aengus much, but I'd been around him enough to know that Ruaraidh was right.

Mairead told me where she lived, out by the ocean, but I'd never been there, or had a car to drive there. So I hired a local taxi to take me to her house Saturday morning. When I got in the car and gave him the address, the driver looked back at me and said, "That's where Mairead lives."

"I know. That's where I'm going."

"You know that's Ailin's wife don't you?" He stared at me through the rear view mirror waiting for a response.

"Yes, I do know that's Ailin's wife. Can you take me there or not?"

"What are you going out there for?

"None of your business. Can you take me there or do I need to take another taxi?"

He smiled at me and said, "Good luck with that."

"Why?"

"Cause I'm the only one in town, ogfhear."

I didn't know what 'ogfhear' meant, but I had a pretty good idea. "Are you going to take me, yes or no?"

"Seven Euro, paid in advance."

I paid him the money and we rode in silence. We arrived at a high stone wall with a wooden gate. I couldn't see any house behind the wall, but the cab stopped and the driver said, "I'm busy the rest of the day. Good luck getting back." As a mild form of protest I left the door open when I got out of the cab. He lurched the car, trying to get the door to close, but it wouldn't. He then stopped the car, got out, shut the door, and yelled something at me that I'm glad I couldn't understand.

The reason I couldn't see a house behind the stone wall was because the land sloped downhill towards the ocean. Her house was near the edge, on a bluff about two hundred feet above the water. Except for wooden frames around the windows and doors, the house was made completely of stone. It was gorgeous and, I'm assuming, very expensive.

Mairead met me at the door wearing a silky, slinky, ankle length dress. When Claire, the Amite, wore something long like this it seemed clunky, geeky, and asexual. Mairead, on the other hand, gave new meaning to the fashion industry's design and objective for this sexy garment.

She had tea prepared. I'd rather have coffee, but the scenery made tea very acceptable. She had a table set in a room where one wall was entirely glass, looking out into the sea. It was stunning. She showed me the entire house, including the bedrooms, which also looked out on the ocean. My mind was going 100 mph as I dreamed of lying in bed with Mairead, looking out into the sea. Suddenly, my dream vanished as she said, "I've got breakfast waiting for us; let's eat."

The smell of bacon permeated the dining room; the aroma was nearly as intoxicating as Mairead. Sort of. I said to her, "I think as long as I have bacon to eat, everything will be okay."

She smiled back at me and said, "Bacon cannot solve all our problems, Mark. That's what beer is for."

The breakfast was incredible and the tea tolerable. The conversation and scenery were beyond description. When she cleared the table and asked me to go sit on the couch near the bay window, I knew we were getting close to the real reason she asked me out here.

I sat on one end of the smallish couch and she brought herself another cup of tea and sat on the other end. At this point everything was still okay and I was in full command of my senses and faculties. However, she took a small sip of tea, then leaned forward to speak to me. When her low-cut dress exposed a little more cleavage than I could process at that moment, I lost concept of time and purpose.

Occasionally, no matter how hard you fight it, the beast inside you seems to win. Sometimes I wrestle with my demons. Sometimes we just snuggle. This was one of those times. To be conscious, I was as unconscious as one could be. Mairead was speaking to me, but I never heard her. I didn't hear anything except the demon inside me. And he wasn't being nice. Finally, "Mark? Are you okay?"

"Yes, I'm sorry, I had something on my mind." Something I could never tell her.

She then said, "I know what you're doing. And I know I can't stop it. I'm just asking you to please take care of Ailin and do whatever you can to see that he doesn't get hurt."

Ailin? Know what we're doing? Not get hurt? Now I'm really confused. "Don't try to deny it," she said, "I have sources. I know you've been with them on some sort of raid. You don't have to tell me what you did, but please don't treat me like a fool and deny it either.

"Just promise me, Mark, that you'll do everything you can to keep Ailin from getting hurt?"

Should I tell her that I'm just a radio-listening, in-the-dark, know-nothing peon? I don't think so. "I'll do my best Mairead, but you should know by now that Ailin is pretty much going to do what Ailin wants to do."

"I know that. Just do whatever you can. That's all I'm asking." A tear formed in her eye, but she quickly wiped it away. She continued, "Mark, our relationship is difficult to understand. Even for Ailin and me, it's not easy. Obviously the incident with the video and the girl was a major issue, but that simply was the culmination of several events and issues between us." As I nodded, she continued her personal story to me, "We had many problems, as all married couples do, but there were a few we didn't know how to repair."

She leaned back on the couch, which made it a bit easier for me to concentrate or her story, and began to give me the long version of their history together. Apparently, Mairead had been an associate professor of Humanities at Trinity College in Dublin, when they met. Ailin had just published his first history of Ireland and was on a book signing tour of colleges and schools around the country. She met him there when she asked him to sign her book for her. According to her, it was "like at first sight."

They went out that night and the next night before he had to continue his tour of colleges. But they were both smitten with each other's appearance, intellect, passion, and acumen. Over the next several months Ailin visited Dublin regularly and they fell madly in love with each other. They went to concerts and the theater and clubs around Dublin and reveled in each other's character and personality.

Ailin begged her to marry him, and Lord knows it was hard to say "no" to Ailin regarding anything. But she was a city girl and she loved the arts and the opportunities in and around Dublin. She didn't have any reservations about marriage—she knew she loved Ailin. She had reservations about leaving the city and moving to the northern hinterlands, to some remote village she'd never heard of, Dungloe. But Ailin's persona and magnetic personality eventually convinced her heart over her mind to marry and abandon the life she had always loved.

The first year or two, they were as happy as anyone could be. Guinevere and King Arthur in their own perfect world, as Ailin saw it. But Guinevere soon became . . . not unhappy, or homesick, or bored, but there was something missing. Life in and around Dungloe was quite different than her life in a university and a metropolitan center like Dublin. Year after year, it weighed on her. She didn't dwell on it, but she knew in her heart something was missing. The video affair with Ailin and the girl enhanced what she already knew.

She started to move back to Dublin that day. But she couldn't. She wanted to divorce Ailin. But she couldn't. She wanted her old life back, but . . .

So, here she is. Not married really. Not divorced either. Not able to leave the man she thinks she still loves, yet still longing to be elsewhere. What does she do? What can she do? And when she asked me that question, I shrewdly kept silent.

We didn't discuss it anymore. Sometimes it's best to leave unpleasantness alone. We sat outside and watched the waves until the rain started again. Then we went inside and spoke of books and ideas and tried to solve all the world's problems. Even though we may have failed at that, she was amazing. And, she's Ailin's wife. And he's my boss and my friend. Did I mention that before?

20

MAIREAD GAVE ME A RIDE back into town and dropped me at the pub. Guess who was sitting on the bench outside the pub? How do I explain this? She waved to Ailin but didn't speak as she drove away. I walked over to him and sat down. He didn't ask anything or say anything. I finally said, "I was going to tell you last night that she invited me up for brunch this morning, but you weren't here. Do you want to hear what happened?"

Without looking up, he replied, "Yes. It's better to get hurt by the truth than comforted with a lie."

I could tell he was troubled and distressed. I also knew the heartache he was feeling was tearing him apart. I first said, "You know it has nothing to do with me, don't you?"

He looked over for the first time and asked, "Truly?"

"Of course not, Ailin, she only needed someone to talk to. She has no one. You must be aware of that."

"I know. I know, and I do trust you. She needs someone to confide in and Lord knows she can't talk to any of the people around here. It's just that sometimes I can feel my bones straining under the weight of all the lives I'm not living."

How do I answer that? By silence. We continued to sit there, reflecting on life and our present situations. Me, hurting for my friend and longing for a certain green-eyed, implausibly magnetic dream. And him, wanting, but not having the one thing in his life he can't have. The one thing all his money and power cannot buy. Love.

After several minutes of silence, he rose and patted me on the shoulder, saying, "Thanks for being my friend. And, thanks for being Mairead's friend as well. She needs you as much as I do." He took a couple of steps, then stopped, turned around, and asked, "Any word from Niamh?" All I could do was shake my head "no."

He kept on walking. I kept holding on to the pink hair clip in my pocket. Dreaming, hoping, wishing for its owner to come back into my life. I looked at the clock in the town center and wondered if was too late to take the bus over to Burtonport today. Any other day, I would've gone in an instant. But Ruaraidh asked me earlier in the week if I could sub for him in the bar this evening. Since he was seldom off, I really couldn't say no.

Ruaraidh was pacing in the pub waiting for me. He quickly said, "Can I leave now?"

"Sure," I answered. "Have you got a big date tonight?"

"Date? No. I'm going out drinking with my boys." I found this very hard to comprehend, since all he did at the pub was drink. Why would he have to go "out" to drink? I know I should have left this alone. I know I should mind my own business. But I couldn't.

So I asked the dumb question, the one question I knew I shouldn't have, "Why do you have to go out to drink?"

He looked quizzically back at me and replied, "Because I need some new stories."

Because I need some new stories? I'm trying to somehow analyze and comprehend what I'm hearing. But before I can ask anything else, he says, "Look, if you don't drink, like you, then all your stories suck and end with 'And then I got home.' Sorry, Mark, but I don't want to be boring like you."

The night in the pub behind the bar was uneventful but entertaining. Pubs in Ireland aren't like bars in America. Back home, the younger crowd tends to get drunker and rowdier as the night goes on. The later it gets, the more shots they drink and the more bouncers you need. It's not like that here. Most pubs are more family oriented and it's not unusual to see kids running around and people of all ages sitting, listening to the music, and talking amongst themselves. Seldom does anyone drink anything other than Guinness. When someone orders a light-colored beer, it causes everyone to stop and stare. Straight shots of liquor are almost unheard of. Birthdays and holidays are reserved for some Irish whiskey, but even that is done in moderation. The heavy drinking is done at home.

❦

I decided I'd take the bus to Burtonport Sunday morning, but I was disappointed. The buses, nor much of anything else, operated on Sunday morning. All good Irishmen and women are in church, or else have the good sense to stay off the streets so others won't see they aren't in church. So I waited.

I finally arrived in Burtonport around half one (1:30 for you Americans), only to find most of the little village closed up. The small pub I'd been in before was open, but no one was inside except an older man behind the bar reading a newspaper. I walked down the street and around the corner to the taxi stand, but the entire street was empty. No taxi, no cars, no people, and everything closed. I walked back to the pub and walked in, surprising the man behind the bar.

"Can I help you?" he asked.

I didn't really want anything to eat or drink, so I asked him, "I'm trying to find a taxi. Do you know where it might be?"

He put the paper down, and said, "We don't have no taxis here, Sonny."

I didn't want to argue with the old guy or make him mad, but I did say, "I was here a week ago and caught the taxi from the stand around the corner. I was wondering where it might be today?"

"Sonny, there ain't no taxi here in Burtonport. Hasn't been for probably seven or eight years."

Quite stupidly I replied, "Are you sure?"

As soon as I asked that question, I knew it was a mistake. He looked fiercely at me and said, "Son, everyone is entitled to be stupid, but don't abuse the privilege."

"But," I protested, "I took the taxi last week. It was open for business. I didn't dream it. Are you absolutely certain it's not running again?"

"Sonny, what's your name?"

"Mark" I answered.

"Mark, the only taxi that's ever been in Burtonport was owned and operated by my uncle, Seamus. He died about seven years ago and there's been no taxi service since then."

"But there's a taxi stand around the corner, and I caught a taxi there last week."

He paused a moment and asked, "Around the corner you say?"

"Yes. The taxi was parked there right in front of the 'For Hire' sign."

"What was the name of the taxi company?" he asked.

I had to think for a few seconds, but I was quite sure the car had no name on it. Nothing at all. "I don't think it had a name or any words on it. I'm pretty sure it was just a normal car."

"Mark, that sign has been up at that spot for over twenty years. My uncle had it put there, cemented in place, and it was just too much trouble to take down when he died. So we left it there. There's no taxi service."

Totally bewildered, I apologized for disturbing him and stumbled outside. I walked down the block and turned the corner, walking towards the 'For Hire' sign. I found a bench and sat down staring at the sign. I instinctively grabbed the pink hair clip from my pocket, just to reassure myself this entire scenario wasn't a dream.

21

IN NORTH CAROLINA, Gina and Charles were living the life. The profits from the sale of her husband's properties, especially the one Walmart bought, allowed them to live large. For the time being, that is. The way Gina was spending, it wouldn't last long. But, if you knew you were going to cash in a two million dollar life insurance policy within the next several months, why not live large? So they did.

Charles continued to work and sue everyone and anyone he could, while Gina bought clothes and planned trips. Her long legs and pretty face were an expensive habit for Charles to afford. But he was hooked and would sue whoever it took to keep Gina happy and in new shoes. He advertised in papers, on city benches, and on the sides of buses around town. He would help you get "what you deserved." And he would only take 40% of your settlement. What a prince.

They were already counting and planning on the insurance money from Paul's death. They only had to convince themselves that he was indeed dead. They would have told all their friends about Paul's body being washed ashore in Virginia, if they had any friends. But their kind didn't have friends. They had people they used, abused, and belittled. Their story, completely fabricated, was only told to business associates, country club debutantes, and themselves, of course, apparently trying to convince each other it was true.

Just about the only thing that could alter their dream was if Paul arose from the dead. Not only would they not get the two million, but they would probably be prosecuted for fraud and insurance scam. And certainly Charles would be disbarred, never to bed the long-legged Gina ever again. He could not, and would not, ever allow this to happen. His own private detective kept working the case of the missing Paul, earching every nook and cranny available in North Carolina and the entire United States. But sadly for them, not Ireland.

22

IT WAS VERY STRANGE for me to have no Halloween or Thanksgiving holidays, especially Thanksgiving, where in the U.S. we normally had four days off. Not here. We just had colder days and less sunlight. Ireland, being so far north, experienced long nights and short days as fall and winter approached. And as the days were shorter and colder, the locals spent more time in the pubs, which was good for our business.

The Amite had gone on vacation, traveling to the south of Portugal for warmer weather. Portugal apparently was, and is, a popular vacation spot for the Irish and much of Europe. It's not as expensive or rude as France, and easier to get to than Italy. Ailin had pre-arranged for Mairead to fill in for Claire while she was on vacation. Mairead loved it and as you can guess, so did I. I spent the next couple of days working in the pub because Ruaraidh was out sick again. I don't know what's going on with him.

With the Amite gone, I'd leave the pub and have lunch every day in the restaurant. Some people are like clouds, once they're gone, it's a beautiful day. But the cloud returned. I stopped by the restaurant Monday morning just to make sure Claire had returned and hadn't been kidnapped and sold into slavery by the Portuguese. I simply opened the door and she saw me and said, "We're not open yet. Come back later . . . or NOT."

Let it go. Walk away and just let it go. I have to keep reminding myself that some people were just raised differently. So I went back to the pub for my morning coffee with Ailin. We sat inside now because it was much too cold to be sitting out on the bench. As I was sitting down, our rather plump waitress brought my coffee and said, "I see Claire's back. I bet you really missed her, didn't you?" And being the good waitress she is, she walked quickly away before I could respond.

Ailin, however, did respond. He said, "You know she's in love with you, don't you?"

I thought he meant the waitress. I said, "Ailin, she's what, 19 years old? And I think she's pregnant as well."

He made sure I met his gaze and lowered his voice saying, "Don't you ever say anything to a woman that even remotely suggests that you think she's pregnant, unless you can see an actual baby emerging from her at that moment."

I told you he was the "smartest man in the world." Then he added, "Not her, eejit, Claire!"

"Claire! You cannot be serious! She hates my guts and can't stand for me to even walk in the restaurant. Just this morning, I . . ."

"Stop," he said, "hold on. I know what she 'says' to you, but you don't know how she 'looks' at you. You're too busy getting flustered and upset. I'd have never thought you'd let a woman get you in such a state."

"She's not a woman. She's a she-devil! And not a pretty one either."

Ailin grinned. I think he was enjoying this. Then he said, "Just don't close the door. She may be something you never dreamed of. Weeds are flowers, too, once you get to know them."

He is my boss and my friend, and I'm pretty sure he's much smarter than me. And I remembered, sometimes silence is a really good answer.

That evening, as Ailin and I sat sipping our evening Guinness, he asked, "Do you want to help us out tomorrow?"

I could hardly believe it. It had been such a while since my first adventure, if you can call it that. I figured they didn't want me any longer. I quickly replied, "Of course. Tell me what do."

"Be ready about half eight and wear some warm clothes." That's all. No other information. He simply nodded and patted me on the shoulder as he started for the steps up to his apartment.

The next morning he didn't come down for his usual tea. I nervously drank my coffee, fidgeting while waiting for half eight. I saw Turlough drive up out front just as Ailin came down the stairs. I wondered if that was just coincidence, IRA precise timing, or did Ailin text him? At any rate, we both went to the car and Turlough drove us out of town where we met the other two guys from the last mission.

Again, I was to drive Ailin's car with all the electronic equipment and follow them to wherever it was we were going. They didn't tell me. I soon noticed that we followed every sign towards Omagh, a small city in Northern Ireland. Anyone who has spent any time in Ireland knows Omagh. This was the city where a car bomb exploded in 1998 killing twenty-nine people and injuring another 220—a sad and tragic day in the history of the IRA and Northern Ireland.

The IRA had planted the bomb but only intended to detonate it as a scare tactic to the Brits, not to injure anyone. However, when they called the British police to tell them about the bomb and its location, about 30 minutes before it was set to explode, panic took over. Confusion reigned and instead of the police herding people away from the car bomb, they unknowingly herded people towards the bomb. And utter disaster ensued. As a result of this catastrophe, the Irish/British peace process began, which ultimately led to the end of physical violence, but not the end of efforts to thwart the British and evict them from Ireland.

As I'm driving along, I'm hoping and praying there are no bombs in my future today. There weren't.

As with the last mission, I was told to monitor the radio and listen for any police activity in our vicinity. We parked the cars on a fairly busy street in the middle of Omagh, and the other four left on foot. I sat in the car and got cold and very bored. I'd occasionally crank the car up and turn the heater on, but I didn't want to draw any unneeded attention so I didn't leave it running very long. Unlike the last mission, which was fairly quick, this one was not.

One hour. Two hours. Three hours. Four hours, and I was about to wet my pants. I'd had a thermos of coffee and a bottle of water to break the boredom and now I seriously had to pee. There was a small pub just down the street, so I tried my best to walk over normally, which was very hard to do. I made it to the restroom successfully, not really garnering any attention, since I didn't speak to anyone. On the way back to the car, there was small newsstand which had books, magazines, and all sorts of snacks available. Since I didn't know how much longer I'd be alone, I decided to buy a couple of magazines and a candy bar.

I handed the guy a 20 Euro note and he just stared at me, then said, "We don't take Euros here."

Stupidly, I hadn't thought about being in Northern Ireland, a part of Britain, where they still use the Pound as currency. I said, "I'm sorry, this is all I have. You sure you can't take it?"

He replied, "Oh, I can take it, but I can't give you any change, I don't have Euros." I told him that was fine, just take the 20 Euro and give me a couple of magazines and a candy bar. He said, "But you'd get a lot of change back. Do you want anything else?" I certainly didn't want another bottle of water, so I told him to just keep the change.

He took the money and bagged up the candy bar and the magazines, then tore off four tickets from the lottery and threw them in the bag saying, "Here, this'll even it out a tad." Fine with me, I just wanted to get back in the car and get warm.

I flipped through the magazines. It was impossible to get away from the Kardashians even in the far reaches of Northern Ireland. Sickening. I ate my candy bar and slid the four lottery tickets in my wallet. Eventually, two and a half hours later, the boys finally come strolling down the street sipping tea and carrying a bag of sandwiches. Ailin hands me a hot cup of tea, which I gladly accepted, and some sort of meat sandwich. I wasn't sure what it was, but it was good.

I again rode back with Turlough, who did not volunteer any information, or even speak to me. He did, however, turn the heater up which after a few minutes put me fast asleep. I didn't wake until we arrived back home at the pub, which is when Turlough spoke for the first time, "We're here."

I must say, this IRA business is about the most boring thing I've ever done—except for maybe watching back-to-back soccer matches.

23

TWO DAYS LATER, Ailin walks up to the table where I'm waiting on him for our evening drink and lays a newspaper in front of me. I look at it, but I'm really not that concerned with school board meetings or the increasing rate of inflation or who won the regional hurling championships last night. I glance at the paper, then back at Ailin, and shrug, asking, "What?"

"Look on page three."

I open the paper and see a small article about the British leader, stationed in Omagh, who is quoted as saying, "I am not a crook!" I look back at Ailin and ask in a whisper, "Did we have something to do with this?"

He only smiles and takes a nice, big drink of his nightly Guinness. I continued reading, but the article was rather short and did not go into much detail. Apparently some funds went missing or were unaccounted for, and this particular British government official who was in charge of the funds can't explain it. His Irish constituents are demanding an inquiry and restitution.

Ailin quickly changes the subject and asks if I have any news of Niamh. I fill him in on my meaningless, worthless trip to Burtonport last week. He asks the same questions I've been asking myself all week none of which I have any answers for. "And you're sure you didn't hear her last name? I have a good friend who lives in the next village over, Annagry, and he probably knows everyone in Burtonport as well. I could ask him to help."

"Ailin, trust me, if I knew her name, or anything at all about her, I'd be over there in a flash."

He says, "Let me work on it, I'll call my friend. Tell me again what she looks like, her age, and the type of car she was driving. If this girl is from Burtonport, he'll know her, especially if she's as pretty as you say she is."

I give him all the information I can think of except how good she kisses and how beautiful her eyes are. He says, "I'll get back with you. Don't give up, but you might want to think about Claire. I understand she's been asking why you haven't come by the restaurant lately."

As I roll my eyes, he puts his hands up and says, "Just a suggestion. See you tomorrow."

The next day I finally relent and go by the restaurant, only because it's my job to check on it. I walk in and don't see Claire anywhere, so I decide to have early dinner before my nightly meeting with Ailin. The winter weather makes it seem much later than it actually is. It starts getting dark around 4:00 PM and the sun doesn't actually rise until about 9:00 AM. It's dark a long time. And, even though the high temperature for the day may be 8 degrees Celsius (or 47 degrees for us Americans), which is not really that cold, it just FEELS much colder with the constant rain and wind.

I order a nice plate of vegetables, meaning potatoes, and leg of lamb. As the food arrives so does the Amite. She walks in the front door, smiles at me, and walks back to the kitchen. Not a word spoken. Miracle. I finish the meal and even have dessert, which is some dish I can't pronounce, but it's a cross between ice cream, caramel and banana pudding. I'm sure it's not very fattening. Then Claire comes from the back, walks up to my table, and says, "Good evening. Was everything satisfactory?" I tell her it was all very nice and she then says, "Thanks for coming in. I hope to see you again soon." I'm thinking, alright, what's going on here?

She looks down at my silence and says, "What?"

So I answer quite honestly and tell her, "Well, this change in your personality towards me is refreshing. Is this the real you?"

She tilts her head upward a bit, looking down her nose at me and replies, "Some people say I'm condescending. That means I talk down to them." As I sit there trying to figure out if she just insulted me or not, she says, "Have a nice day," and walks away smiling.

❦

The next Saturday, a cold and blustery day, I take the bus back to Burtonport. To do what? I don't know, maybe in the possibility of accidentally or providentially running into Niamh again. I hold on to the hair clip, which hasn't left my pocket since that day on the cliff, and hope for the best. My first stop is again at the only pub in town. Fortunately for me, the older man from before is not here this morning. There's only one other person in the bar, except for the middle-aged, overweight woman behind the counter.

The other customer is at the far end with his arms crossed on the bar and his head laid down on them with his eyes closed. I don't know if he's actually asleep, or somehow, this early in the morning, passed out. At any rate, he doesn't move. The lady behind the bar smiles and welcomes me, offering coffee before I even sit or order anything. From my first day in Ireland, I've been amazed at the friendliness, geniality, and neighborliness of the people.

I accept a cup of coffee and her conversation, which is mostly about the weather. I'm sure she can tell I'm not from Ireland, but she doesn't ask. She just smiles and refills my cup. After I've heard the stories about how cold it was last year and about the deep snow they had four years ago, I get up the nerve to ask her if she knows a young lady named Niamh. She tilts her head a little, closes one eye, then asks, "What's her last name?" Sadly and tragically, I still don't know the answer to that. She apologizes and tells me she doesn't know anyone with that name. She used to know an older woman named Niamh years ago, but she died of the gout.

"Are you sure there's no young ladies with that name living here?" I ask, hoping for a miracle.

"Quite sure lad, I've lived here my entire life and there're only 731 of us left here now. And, I'm related to most of them."

That surprised me. Not that she's related to all of them, but that there are only 731 people in the village. I had no idea it was so small; it seemed larger. She volunteered more information: "We used to be bigger, but the fishing industry has been going downhill for years. The large companies have all but driven the smaller fishermen out. We just can't compete. We still have a few boats going out from here, but nothing like the old days. Most of the stores and building you see are closed now, it's really sad for us."

Then she brightened up a bit and asked, "So who is this Niamh you're looking for, if you don't mind me asking?" I didn't mind at all. I told her the entire story except, of course, how well she kissed. I even showed her the hair clip, just so she wouldn't think I had fabricated the entire event.

She smiled and said, "I'll keep an eye out for her. Would you like me to call you if I see her?" Of course I would. I need all the help I can get. I gave the number of the pub in Dungloe and told her I could be reached there.

When she heard that she asked, "Well then, you probably know Ailin, don't you?"

"Yes ma'am, I do. He's a good friend and, in fact, I'm working for him."

She smiled and winked at me saying, "Tell him Kathleen says hello and to keep up the good work."

I leave the pub and walk around the corner to the "For Hire" sign, but it's too cold today to sit outside and stare at it. I keep moving but there's really nothing else to see. Kathleen was right, most of the businesses have closed up. There's a petrol station at the end of the street and I walk in just to get out of the wind for a bit. A young guy is behind the counter, reading The Picture of Dorian Gray. He looks up and nods and asks, "Where's your car?"

"I took the bus over," I tell him.

He lowers the book and says, "Why?" It would take too long to explain it all to him, so instead, I just tell him I was looking for a young lady named Niamh hoping he might know her.

He asks, "Did you find her?"

"No, I didn't. Just bad luck I guess."

He looks at me rather seriously and replies, "You never know what worse luck your bad luck saved you from."

This rather sage advice from an Irish teenager, reading an Oscar Wilde novel, somehow did not surprise me. I thank him and wish him a grand day and walk back into town to the bus stop. Maybe it was just a dream. Maybe those incredible green eyes were simply an illusion. Maybe this pink hair clip with little hearts on it is a fabrication of my imagination. Hopefully, not.

24

THE MAN BEHIND the counter at the bus station/grocery store in Burtonport tells me the next bus won't be around for about an hour. I'll have to wait. There's a bench inside, out of the cold, so I buy bottle of juice and a pastry and start watching the small television he has on. Their TV is not much different from ours, except for all the soccer.

During halftime of the soccer match, the major news story airing is about someone who won 287,500 Pounds in the lottery in Northern Ireland but hasn't come forward to claim it. The lottery all over Ireland and Britain is fairly common. What's not common is for someone to win and not claim the winnings. That made news!

With my mouth full of pastry, it dawns on me that I was in Northern Ireland and a clerk gave me a few lottery tickets. What did I do with them? I remember, I put them in my wallet. Then when I got home, I threw them in the top drawer of my dresser. As I'm recalling this incident, the winning lottery numbers are shown on the TV screen. I try to remember them but it's impossible; they're gone before I can fix them in my mind. When I asked the clerk if he saw the numbers, he replied, "No, I don't mess with that rubbish."

I bought a local newspaper and searched for the winning lottery numbers, but it only showed this week's winnings. I look back at the television and the interminable soccer match has started again. I'm a little excited. It's possible that I won, isn't it? It could happen. The bus finally arrives. I board and can't wait to get back to the apartment to check my tickets.

I race upstairs, not taking my coat or hat off, and excitedly open the top drawer. There they are, my four tickets from that day in Omagh. And I then realize, I don't know what the winning numbers are. My tickets could be as worthless as piece of cabbage. Dang!

The computer, yes. I fire it up, but we don't have high speed internet service here, as in America, so I wait. And I wait. I'm pretty sure my hair has grown another inch before it finally responds. I Google "lottery" and get about five hundred different options. Then I narrow it down to "lottery in Northern Ireland" and still get dozens of options. Finally, I type in "unclaimed lottery winnings in Britain." Boom! There it is, the complete story, with the winning numbers. I try to read the article, but after I see the part where it says, "The winning ticket was sold from a vendor in Omagh," I can't read anymore.

I leap over to the dresser, grab my four tickets, and spring back to the computer. I scroll down to the winning numbers. I look at the first ticket . . . No. The second ticket . . . No. Sweat instantly pops out on my forehead as I look at the third ticket . . . 6, 11, 17, 18, 29, and the superball number, 14.

Jesus, Mary, and Joseph! I've won the lottery! I've won the lottery! That's all I can say, it's all I can think . . . I've won the lottery! What to do? Holy cow Mark, or Paul, or whatever my name is . . . what do I do?

I look at the winning ticket and read all the fine print on both sides. It's good for up to six months after the lottery. Great, I don't have to worry about that. Then, in fine print it instructs anyone who "thinks" they've won anything to call this number for verification and instructions. I call. Instead of the lottery office, I get my landlord, Mrs. O'Leary, downstairs. "Hello, Mrs. O'Leary, I'm trying to make a phone call."

"Who are you trying to call?"

"It's personal, can you please get off the line?"

"No, I can't, because you're dialing long distance. You can make local calls here, but you can't call long distance without me approving it."

"Okay, can you please approve it so I can make the call?"

"Are you going to pay me for the expense?"

"Of course, I'm going to pay you. Don't you trust me?

"My last tenant ran off still owing me."

"I'll be down in twenty seconds to pay you in advance for the call."

"No, I'll trust you this time, Mark. You're not calling a prostitute are you?"

"No, ma'am, I'm not calling a prostitute."

"Okay, because if you'd just make up with Claire, she'd make you a good wife."

"What? Claire?" Calm down, don't go there, just say okay and hang up. "Okay, Mrs. O'Leary, thank you."

Finally. I call the number and they put me on hold. I wait. And wait. Then a woman comes on the line and I tell her I think I've won the lottery. She says, "Which lottery?" I tell her the one that no one has claimed. She asks me if I have the ticket with me, which I do, and to read the numbers for her. Which I do. She then asks me where I bought it; I tell her in Omagh. She asks if I live there; I tell I was only visiting, that I live in Dungloe, hoping that won't be a problem.

"No problem," she says, "I just need your name and address and for you to bring the winning ticket to our office so we can verify to make sure it's not a fake." Great! I give her my name and address and she tells where to come. The closest lottery office is in Londonderry which, as I remember, is not that far.

After I hang up with the lottery office, I'm so excited it's impossible to sit still, so I start for the pub. I, however, do have enough common sense about me to thoroughly understand NOT TO TELL ANYONE about this.

I have the lottery ticket safely inside my wallet, next to the pink hair clip, in my front pants pocket, not back. I put my hand in the pocket as well and hold on to my two prized possessions, suddenly wondering which one is actually more important to me. Before I'm forced to answer this, Ruaraidh greets me from afar, "Where've you been all day?"

I answer with a simple, "Out."

I order a pint, which seemed to make Ruaraidh very happy, and he said, "Ahh, alcohol, the cause and solution to all life's problems."

I asked if he'd seen Ailin around this evening. He told me Ailin came in early, drank a pint, and went upstairs. Dang, I really need to talk to him about this. He's the only person I can trust. I can't decide whether to wait till tomorrow or go up the stairs to his apartment and knock on the door. I've never been upstairs before. I've never even seen anyone go upstairs before. I can either sit here like a nervous cat, I can continue talking with Ruaraidh, or I can do the unthinkable and go upstairs and knock on Ailin's door.

Let me narrow that down to two things I can do. My head is starting to hurt. I've almost decided to finish my pint and go back home for the night when Ruaraidh walks back over to me and says, "Stop thinking so much; it's alright not to know all the answers."

Before I can respond, Ailin puts his hand on my shoulder. I turn and see him as he says, "You were looking for me?" I look back at Ruaraidh, he smiles and walks away.

"Can I talk to you about something important?"

As I knew he would, he says, "Come over here and let's sit down." I bring my pint with me and ask Ailin if he wants anything. He answers, "No, I don't usually drink this late." After we sit, I tell him the whole story starting with the day in Omagh and my getting the lottery tickets, till now, when I walked in the pub.

He waves at Ruaraidh and orders a whiskey. I've never seen Ailin drink whiskey. We wait in silence until Ailin gets his drink and then he downs it in one shot. He looks at me and says, "You're in trouble."

"No," I assure him, "I won't be crazy spending it. I know some people would buy cars and boats and all sorts of stuff, but I'm not going to do that."

He orders another whiskey, waits for Ruaraidh to bring it over and leave, then says, "I know you're not, because you're not going to take the money. You're going to give it back."

If he'd been speaking Mandarin Chinese, with a Russian accent, I would have understood him better than the statement he just made.

25

CERTAINLY, Ailin is not jealous of the money I won. He has considerably more than that. Why is he saying I'm in trouble? My head is spinning trying to figure out what is happening between us. He senses I'm confused and begins, "Listen, if you go collect that money at the lottery office, they're going to take your picture and it'll be in the papers. Next, you'll have to fill out forms so they can deduct taxes from the winnings. Third, you'll have to verify your identity to them."

I sat stunned and suddenly very confused. I have no legal identity, all I have is a made-up name. I have no records of my entry into this country or any records to even show that I exist. And I certainly don't want my picture plastered in the papers. I could be deported, arrested, exposed, or anything in between. I looked back at Ailin and said, "I have totally screwed up."

He nodded and said, "Yep."

After several moments he continued, "We can fix this. But you cannot take the money. It would've been a lot better if you hadn't told them your name and address, but we can work with that as well. First thing tomorrow you call them back and tell them you're anonymously donating the money to charity. I'm not sure how it all works, but if they insist you sign for it, so they can get their taxes done properly, just refuse it all and tell them to keep it. Tell them the tickets you got were given to you and that your religious beliefs prevent you from accepting money from gambling."

He ordered another whiskey, downed it in one gulp, and told me to go back home and call the lottery office first thing in the morning. He added a warning: "Call from HERE! Don't use the phone at Mrs. O'Leary's." He then told me we'd be alright. He went back upstairs, but it was impossible for me to move anywhere.

After several minutes, or hours, I don't know which, Ruaraidh came to my table and said, "I don't want to know what happened. I've never, ever seen Ailin drink whiskey, so whatever it was that caused him to drink, I don't want to know. But I do want you to understand that no matter what it was, I'll help if I can."

I looked up at this big oaf and said, "We'll be friends forever, won't we Ruaraidh?"

He looked back and replied, "Even longer."

It was a fretful night trying to sleep. My only saving grace was holding the hair clip in my hand and trying to think emerald thoughts instead of financial ones. Ailin is waiting for me at the pub to give me support this morning when I arrive. I make the call to the lottery office and explain to the lady that I don't want the money. I ask them to please donate it to charity. She says, "You still have to accept it. It's technically not our money any longer. You accept it, have the taxes taken out, and then you can donate it to whoever you choose."

A few seconds of silence, then the lady says, "Are you still there Mr. McCarty?"

Crap! They know my name. Why did I tell them my name? I say, "Hold on a second."

I turn to Ailin and tell him what's happening. He says, "Tell her you refuse to have anything to do with the money. It's against your religious beliefs to touch money from gambling and you won't be tainted with it. If she's a good Catholic girl, she'll understand."

I repeat this to the lady and she seems quite flustered, but eventually says, "This is all quite unusual, but if it is indeed your wishes, then we'll put the money back in the pot for the next drawing. First, however, you must sign a release form, absolving us from any future litigation." She says they can fax it right over or mail it. I ask her to fax it to the pub's office so I can end this whole affair as quickly as possible.

They send it. I sign it and fax it back and immediately feel as though I can breathe again. Ailin gets us tea and coffee and we sit by ourselves, each thinking how lucky I have been. This could've been disaster. Ailin says, "You're probably the luckiest and unluckiest man I've ever met." We have a second cup and then he leaves for the day. I'm left to decompress and try to get my nerves to settle down.

The rest of the day is as normal and unexceptional as possible. I make all the usual rounds, talk to all the regulars, and end the day waiting to have a pint with Ailin this evening. He, however, calls Ruaraidh and tells him he won't be in tonight. Is he with Mairead? Some undercover IRA business? Or, just glad to get away from me for a bit?

As Ruaraidh and I are talking, we hear a commotion by the door. Something is going on outside. Since it's time for me to leave anyway, I grab my coat and start that way to find out what the trouble is. As I open the door, a bright light shines in my face and someone says, "Are you Mark McCarty?" Shielding my eyes and trying to figure out what is happening, I answer, "Yes, what's this about?"

"Are you the man who refused to accept over 287,000 Pounds in lottery winnings?" A young woman is now pressing a microphone in my face and the lights are nearly blinding me. All I can think to say is, "Leave me alone!" I retreat into the bar and shut the door. The young lady and cameraman try to enter, but Ruaraidh comes to my rescue by standing in the doorway and announcing that the pub is closed.

After several fruitless tries to get me to come out and talk to them, they finally give up and load up the cameras and drive away. I'm flabbergasted. The lottery office must've notified the local television station that someone "refused" to accept over 287,000 Pounds. Winning that amount would probably never make the news, but someone WINNING it and REFUSING it was big news.

The next evening, back in North Carolina, Gina is sipping a glass of red wine. Even though she's not overly fond of it, she thinks it makes her more sophisticated. She has her satellite TV tuned in to a rerun of the BBC show Absolutely Fabulous. Again, she assumes that by watching British television, she will assimilate some culture.

At the final commercial break, there is a news flash. Gina thinks it might be about a terrorist bombing, so she continues watching. But it's not about a bombing; it's a human interest story about a man who won a lottery but didn't want the money. The newscaster explained the entire story before a five second clip aired showing the man, named Mark McCarty, standing in front of a bar saying, "Leave me alone!"

Gina was astonished and overwhelmed! If it weren't for the long hair and goatee, this Mark McCarty fellow could have been her ex-husband's twin. Then, reality set in, as she thought, "Was that Paul? Is he in England?" She immediately called her husband, Charles, who was working late as always, and told him what she'd seen. He thought it to be too much of a coincidence and knew of his wife's penchant for red wine lately. So he just sluffed it off and left it to the effects of alcohol. But Gina had a very strong suspicion.

She watched the BBC the rest of the night, but that news item never repeated. She Googled "BBC" but couldn't find anything there. She then Googled "Lottery in England" and kept narrowing it down to "Unclaimed lottery winners in England," until she found the story. But it had no picture. It simply told of a man named Mark McCarty, from Dungloe, Ireland, who won the lottery, but didn't want the money. And Gina thought to herself, "Why would anyone who looks exactly like my ex-husband not want all that money?" She knew why. Now she had to convince Charles why.

They hired a private detective and explained what they wanted. He was successful in obtaining footage of the news flash about the lottery winner. Together, the three of them looked at it over and over. They ran it in slow motion and in stop frame. It certainly "could" have been Paul. The voice was similar, but there just weren't enough words spoken to be sure. Charles wasn't convinced. Gina was mostly convinced. The private detective wanted to go to Ireland and check it all out. Big payday for him. They talked late into the night before deciding that it would indeed be beneficial to ensure this Mark McCarty guy was not Paul. They had two million reasons to make sure it wasn't Paul. Their private detective would leave in a couple of days.

26

AT MY MORNING COFFEE and tea meeting with Ailin, the lottery was obviously the main subject of conversation. I jokingly said, "The next time I win the lottery, I'll know better."

But Ailin still saw the seriousness in the whole affair. He replied, "Sometimes there is no next time, no time-out, no second chance. Sometimes it's now or never. I hope this wasn't one of those."

As the waitress was refilling our cups, she said, "I saw you on the telly this morning. Did you win the lottery?" Oh no, this is not good. Ailin asked her to explain, and she did. The TV "interview" from last night was airing with the story of "The Man Who Turned Down the Lottery." Ailin told me we needed to fix this immediately. I agreed.

Ailin said he would personally go around to each business in town and tell them all that the television report they were seeing wasn't accurate. Our story would be that I had indeed won a lottery in Northern Ireland, but that I didn't know I'd won it until after the expiration date. When I tried to claim it, they told me it was invalid because I'd waited too long. Simple enough, and blaming it on the Brits was something most people in Dungloe would believe. And in order to prevent any more news people from sticking their noses in, Ailin also instructed EVERYONE in town that should they meet anyone looking for me, Mark, they should tell them I moved to London. That was our story and we were sticking with it. Ailin and I both felt the whole thing would fade away in a day or two. Ailin had other "things" to do. So as he was leaving, he said to me, "Tomorrow becomes yesterday quicker than you may think." I hope so.

I knew I would have to field questions from everyone around town for a day or two until people forgot about it. I was prepared for it and it really wasn't that bad. I just blamed it on the Brits and people liked that. The one exception was, of course, the Amite. Somehow, I just knew it wouldn't go well with her. I went in the restaurant to order coffee and a piece of pie, and she walks up to my table. She says, "The secret of life is honesty and fair dealing. If you can fake that, you've got it made."

I look up at the tightly wound bun and the floor length dress and say, "Do you think I've been dishonest with you?"

"Well, let me see," she starts, "you lied about being a Canadian. You lied about your name. It's not Mark is it? You lied about your wild story getting ambushed at the border. And now you're lying about this whole lottery thing. So, yes, you are being dishonest with me."

How can I argue with someone who's right? Even if that someone is the Amite? So, I say, "Claire, you don't see things as they truly are; you see things as you are. We all eat lies when our hearts are hungry." As she's attempting to assimilate these statements of mine, I take a big bite of pie and leave the table before she can respond.

I almost make it to the door when she says to me, "If I agreed with you, we'd both be wrong."

That evening, during our nightly drink, I told Ailin that Claire might be a problem. "Why? What sort of problem?" He asked.

"Well, to start with, she hates my guts. And she's pretty sure my story is completely fabricated."

"Don't worry about Claire. She's only mad because you haven't asked her out like everyone else has. All the other guys in town have, at one time or another, asked her out—except you. She probably resents that. If you go ahead and ask her for a date, then let her turn you down, she'll probably be okay."

I asked, "Why would you think she'd turn me down?"

He took a small drink of Guinness and replied, "Time heals almost everything. Give time, time."

I had no idea what that meant, especially its relevance to me asking Claire out on a date. So I said, "No, really. Tell me why you think she'd turn me down."

So he responds, "Mark, when you fish for love, bait with your heart, not with your brain." Before I could ask what he meant, he continues, "I have some information on your mystery girl, Niamh."

Just hearing the name "Niamh" made me forget anything Amish and turn my full attention to his information. "Go ahead," I say, as I hold my breath and hope for a miracle.

"My friend in Annagry called me back. He knows most everyone in Burtonport and he tells me there's definitely no taxi service there. And as far he can tell, there's no young ladies named Niamh there either. I'm sorry, I know this is not what you wanted to hear."

"I just don't understand, Ailin. I didn't dream this up. I rode with a girl named Niamh. I talked to her. I kissed her. I did not imagine all this!"

He took a deep breath and said, "I know. I can't explain it either. Burtonport is just a small fishing village. Everyone knows everyone, my friend included. And if there was a pretty girl living there, no matter what her name was, he'd know her."

I gripped the pink hair clip in my pocket a little tighter and asked, "Well, should I just give up? I don't know what else to do?"

Ailin nodded thoughtfully, then told me, "Maybe it won't work out. But, maybe seeing if it does will be the best adventure ever. Don't give up yet. I'll talk to my friend again."

Ailin went upstairs and I sat dejectedly in the corner, nursing the same Guinness I've had in my hands now for nearly two hours. As happy as I was a few weeks ago, now I'm the opposite of that. Niamh seems to be as elusive as whoever it was that shot President Kennedy. My lottery dream went up in smoke. And apparently the Amite wants to decline my invitation for a date that I'm never going to ask her on.

Ruaraidh ambles over and asks if I want a fresh drink. "No, thanks. I'm just not feeling very good tonight."

He looks at me and says, "The lottery thing?"

"No," I honestly tell him, "not the lottery."

"Well, it must be a girl then."

No use lying about it to my new friend now. "Yeah, it's a girl . . . NOT CLAIRE!"

"Is she pretty?"

"Very pretty."

"But it's not working out for you?"

"Unfortunately, it's not."

Then Ruaraidh leans down and puts his hands on the table, while staring directly in my eyes and says, "A wise man once told me that no matter how HOT she is, somebody, somewhere, is sick of her." Then he knocks twice on the table and walks away.

❧

The private detective Gina and Charles hired, Herbert Elkins, just landed at the Dublin airport. Soon, he would be wishing he'd flown into Shannon instead of Dublin, where the traffic is like it is in all big cities—terrible. Before he left the airport itself, he'd almost run into two other cars, trying to familiarize himself with driving on the left hand side of the road, while also changing gears with his left hand. He curses Charles for arranging him a "cheap" rental car with manual transmission. It's a long, tiring drive from Dublin to Dungloe.

27

AILIN CALLS HIS FRIEND in Annagry again to ask more questions about the elusive Niamh. His friend, again, tells Ailin that he knows almost everyone in Burtonport, and he's positive there is no woman living there named Niamh. Ailin sighs in discouragement and his friend asks if he should check any other towns for a girl named Niamh. Ailin, thinking that would be pointless, starts to say no and hang up, but replies, "What do you mean by 'other towns'?"

His friend says, "If you want me to, I could check in Bunbeg, Derrybeg, Glenties, other small towns around. I'm sure I could find someone named Niamh in one of them. After all, it's a fairly common name. We've even got one here."

That startles Ailin, and he asks, "You've got what there?"

"We have a girl named Niamh here. In Annagry."

Ailin is flabbergasted! "Why didn't you tell me you knew a girl named Niamh there?"

"Because," he says, "you were looking for a girl in Burtonport, not in Annagry."

Ailin knew the two towns were only seven or eight miles apart. He asks his friend, "Is this Niamh in Annagry a pretty girl?"

"Oh, yes, she's a looker alright, but she's sort of off the market, if you know what I mean."

Ailin says, "No, I don't know what you mean. Is she married?

"Oh, no. She's not married."

"Well, what? Is she gay?"

"I don't think she's gay. No, she couldn't be gay. She has a little girl."

Ailin, totally doesn't understand what his friend is trying to tell him. "Well, why do you say she's off the market then?"

"Because, Ailin, her husband was killed in a boating accident and it's not appropriate for her to be seeing anyone."

"Oh," Ailin replies, "I'm so sorry to hear that. How long ago was he killed?"

"It'll be four years in the spring."

Ailin asks, "Four years you say?"

His friend replies, "Yes, I remember it like it was yesterday, terrible accident."

Ailin repeats, "But it was nearly four years ago?"

"Yes, I told you that. Why?"

"Don't you think that's a pretty long time not to start your life again?"

His friend is silent a few moments, and finally says, "Well, I thought it might be a long time as well, but I asked her out last summer and she said no."

"Did she tell you she was still grieving?"

"No, she just said she wasn't interested."

"Well, you eejit, maybe it was just YOU she didn't want to date!"

His friend was momentarily silent, then said, "I don't think that's possible, Ailin. All the girls like me."

Ailin replies, "I've seen some of the girls who like you. Trust me, it's possible. Tell me what happened to her husband."

"He was out on one of the fishing boats from Burtonport on a regular summer day, no bad weather, nothing out of the ordinary. They were ready to come back to port and were raising the last net when one of the cables snapped. They don't know if the catch was too large or if the cable just snapped from old age. But either way, it snapped and whipped backwards in the boat where he was standing. The cable caught him midsection and cut him in half. Literally, cut him in half. Two pieces."

Ailin thought he might have remembered reading about this years ago. "And his wife has a daughter?"

"Yes, I think she may have been one or two when her dad died. She's a pretty little thing now, just starting school I think."

Ailin's mind was whirling. He asked his friend to once again describe this girl to him. Yes, it had to be the same Niamh that Mark met. He told his friend to say nothing of this conversation to anyone, especially to Niamh. He thanked him and told him to come see him soon. His friend knew this meant Ailin would reward him for the information.

Before Ailin got Mark's hopes up, he wanted to further check the entire Niamh story out for himself. The following day he drove over to Annagry and, as all good Irishmen do, went to the local pub first. It was easy enough to start a conversation with the bored bartender, who told him the same story his friend did about the fishing accident. Ailin probed deeper, asking about Niamh. The bartender told Ailin that he was sure Niamh hadn't remarried, but that several locals had tried to marry her.

Ailin remarked, "She must be a real beauty then, if everyone wants to marry her."

"Oh, she is that, but it's not the reason all the fellows want her so badly. They want her because of her money."

This surprised Ailin. He knew people in this region of Ireland didn't have money. There was no industry, no opportunities, nothing but fishing and sheep herding really. Before he could think of a way to ask further questions, without seeming too nosy, the bartender volunteered exactly what Ailin was looking for. "She got a boatload of money from the insurance settlement when her husband died. More than she and her little girl could ever spend. That's why some of these loafers around here want to marry her so badly. They all want to get their grubby hands on all that cash, then lay up in here all day and drink themselves to death."

Ailin didn't argue; he was sure that was the truth. He still had one other test to make. He had Niamh's address from his friend, so he drove just out of town to a new looking, brick house overlooking a stream and small lake. He pulled in the driveway, walked up to the front of the house and knocked on the door. He stepped back a bit, as not to be threatening. When the door opened, a young lady about thirty years of age, slim, with short, light brown hair tinged with red stood before him. She had a beautiful face and the most gorgeous green eyes Ailin had ever seen. She said, "Can I help you?"

For a quick moment, Ailin was overcome with her eyes and facial features. He recovered saying, "I think I'm a bit lost, can you direct me to the quickest way back to Burtonport?" She gave him the directions and he pretended to be listening to them. But he wasn't. He was now realizing why this emerald-eyed beauty had affected Mark so deeply. He thanked her for her help and returned to his car. He now had to decide how he was going to break this news to his friend.

Herbert Elkins eventually made his way to Dungloe after getting lost enumerable times. Even the newest GPS still has trouble with the winding, twisting, turning roads of rural Ireland. He arrived late afternoon, drove through the town, and decided to go back out of town to a bed and breakfast he had seen a few miles before. No need to raise any suspicion right away.

He was sure it would be a rather simple job to verify, or not, the identity of one Mark McCarty. He thought he'd accomplish that task the next morning and then spend a couple of days touring the scenic Irish countryside—at the expense of Gina and Charles, of course. He knocked on the door of the B&B and a sweet looking older lady answered. He asked her if she had a room available for a night or two.

She looked out at his car, then back at him, and asked, "Where's your wife?"

"I'm not married," He said.

"So, you're quite alone then?"

"Yes, ma'am, I am."

She nodded, then said, "We don't allow orgies and sex parties in my house!"

Startled, Herbert said, "What?"

"I read about you Americans and your party life. I won't have it here."

"I understand, ma'am. There won't be any women coming here, I can assure you."

She nodded again and said, "No men either! You're not that way are you?"

"No, ma'am, just me. I promise."

He checked into his room, and after filling out a travel expense (fudged a bit), he decided to go into town for dinner. He saw two choices, a pub and a restaurant. He chose the restaurant. All he wanted was to have a nice meal, maybe with a nice bottle of wine, since Charles and Gina were paying for it, and then start his investigation tomorrow.

He sat by himself studying the menu when a plain, young woman, with her hair tied in a bun, wearing a long dress came to his table. "Can I help you sir?" It took Claire about three seconds to realize she had another American in her restaurant. He asked about the lamb chops and what kind of wine they served. She replied in a combination of Gaelic and heavy Irish accent, that she was certain no American could ever understand. He couldn't.

He asked more questions and her accent became more pronounced. Ailin had warned them of outsiders coming around asking questions about Mark. She was taking no chances of making Ailin mad at her. Herbert finally just pointed at something on the menu and Claire nodded at him and returned to the kitchen. After a suitable few minutes, she returned with a big slice of rhubarb pie and a side order of stewed cabbage, with warm milk to drink. Herbert decided a nice piece of apple pie would do just fine.

Claire immediately called Ailin with the news of a strange American in town. Ailin was planning to talk with Mark tonight about the news of Nimah. His plans were changed now. By the time Ailin got to the restaurant, Herbert was gone. So, instead, he went around town again, reminding everyone that they give no information out to any strangers. And if asked specifically about Mark, they should say he had moved to London.

28

AILIN CALLED MARK and told him to stay home all day. Strange Americans just don't show up in Dungloe alone, for no reason. Luckily for Herbert, he had a nice breakfast at the B&B and didn't have to return to the restaurant. He was perceptive enough to visit the pub first after breakfast. If anyone knew Mark McCarty, it would be those in the local pub. He was acting like an American tourist and trying not to be so very conspicuous. He failed miserably.

He sat at the bar and ordered a mimosa. Ruaraidh said, "A what?"

Herbert repeated himself, "A mimosa."

Ruaraidh asked, "Is that some kind of new beer?"

Herbert wasn't sure if the bartender was joking with him or just stupid. But he didn't want to offend him, so he said, "Maybe I'll just have a cup of coffee."

Ruaraidh poured the coffee, and having been warned by Ailin of strangers, he kept oddly silent. Herbert finally spoke saying, "I'm looking for an old school friend of mine named Mark McCarty. Do you know him?"

Ruaraidh stared back at him and replied, "Never heard that name before. Any other questions?"

Herbert could tell he'd get nowhere here, so he said, "It seems as if I've put you in a bad mood this morning, so I'll pay my bill and be leaving."

Ruaraidh said, "I thought I was in a bad mood, but it's been a few years, so I guess this is who I am now."

Herbert was perceptive enough to realize he should say no more and leave as quietly as possible. He tried the general store next. Nothing. The post office, the gas station, and the feed store all had the same answers . . . no one had ever heard of Mark McCarty. Herbert knew this was more than a little odd. A local man winning a lottery, then refusing the money and not a single person in town knows him?

His last stop was the restaurant. He was hoping he wouldn't have the same waitress as yesterday. He was disappointed. Claire took his order and brought him coffee and pie, asking him, "Will that be all?"

Herbert nodded, adding, "I'm trying to find my old friend Mark McCarty. Do you know where I might find him?"

Claire told him, "I heard he ran off to London with some floozy. Good riddance I say. He was nothing but a loafer and a drunk for the last twenty years."

Herbert finished his pie and left. Claire called Ailin. Herbert walked around town asking several locals the same question and getting the same two answers: they don't know any Mark McCarty or he's moved to London. Herbert hasn't been a successful private detective for twenty-five years without being a bit discerning and insightful. He knew he was being stonewalled, but he didn't know what to do about it. He figured if he just kept asking people, sooner or later he'd find someone who would slip up and admit something.

Several people called Ailin, as Claire did, keeping him updated on Herbert's progress. Ailin was also insightful enough to understand that sooner or later someone WOULD slip up and say something. He determined that someone should be him. He walked outside the pub and sat on the bench pretending to be reading the paper. In reality, he was waiting for Herbert. He didn't have to wait long. Ailin also knew Herbert wouldn't stop until he found something.

As Herbert strolled by, Ailin stood and asked him, "I understand you're searching for Mark McCarty. Is that true?"

"Yes," a surprised Herbert said, "do you know him?"

Ailin said, "Of course I do, and I can take you to him if you'd like."

Herbert couldn't believe his good fortune, "Yes I would. Are you sure it wouldn't be an imposition? You can just tell me where he is and I'll find him myself."

Ailin smiled and said, "Oh, you'd never be able to find his place on your own. It's out of town with lots of turns. I'll take you there, no problem." They both got in Ailin's car and drove out of town to a peat field in the country. Ailin was pretty sure the American had never seen a peat field before and wouldn't know what he was looking at. The mounds of peat had been recently cut and were piled up in stacks about three feet high, sitting there to dry out. The peat was, of course, black as night and had an earthy, sinister aroma about it. It reminded your senses of something dead.

Ailin stopped the car and asked Herbert to get out. They both stood silent for a few moments and Ailin said, "Do you know what you're looking at?"

Herbert replied, "No, sir I don't, but I'm guessing it's not Mark McCarty."

"No, it's not. It's the people who crossed Mark McCarty."

Herbert said, "I don't understand what you mean."

Ailin then explained, "I'm going to tell you this once. Then we're leaving here and you're leaving town. Mark McCarty is the most powerful IRA boss in the north of Ireland. You don't mess with him. You don't ask questions about him. You don't even acknowledge his existence. The people in town know that. These burial mounds you see here are the people who never learned that lesson." Herbert's head snapped towards Ailin in complete surprise.

Ailin said, "Get in the car, leave this place, and don't ever come back. And most importantly, don't ever ask any questions."

Herbert replied, "I'm not sure I really believe you."

Ailin looked sternly at him and said, "Then tell me why someone would win a big lottery and turn down the money? He doesn't need the money and he doesn't need the publicity. That's why. You can either take my advice or end up here. It's your choice."

They drove back to town in silence. Ailin wasn't sure if Herbert believed his story. Herbert wasn't sure either, but he knew he really didn't want to test it. Ailin dropped Herbert at his car and Herbert drove away. Ailin followed at a distance until he was certain Herbert had left, but he was not convinced Herbert truly believed. He had another phone call to make.

Ailin went back to his office and called North Carolina. He was fortunate to find his own private detective answering the phone. "Desmond Jones, can I help you?"

"Yes, Desmond, it's Ailin calling from Ireland. Can you talk?"

"Yeah, Ailin. What's up?"

"I have a problem with a friend of yours and I need your help."

Surprised, Desmond asked, "A friend of mine? Who would that be?"

"Herbert Elkins. I Googled his name and found he's from your hometown, Winston-Salem. He's over here asking questions he shouldn't be asking."

Desmond had to reassure himself he'd heard correctly: "Herbert Elkins is in Ireland asking questions?"

"Yes. The type of questions I don't want answered. This is why I need your help."

Desmond said, "As long as it's not anything illegal, you know I'll help you."

This is what Ailin told Desmond to do: Buy a cheap, wooden casket and wait till late at night. Then put the casket in front of Herbert Elkins' office so he'll see it when he arrived at work. Put a note inside the casket reading, "From your friends in the IRA, in case you ever need to use it."

Desmond asked, "Is the IRA over here? In North Carolina?"

"No, nowhere close. But he doesn't have to know that. Can you take care of it? If so, send me the bill for everything."

Desmond said, "Yeah, I'll take care of it. He must be working for that lawyer, Charles, trying to find out some information for the life insurance policy."

Ailin responded, "I thought so, too."

Desmond then asked, "Your friend is still dead, isn't he?"

"Of course he is, Desmond. Why would you ask such a silly question?"

Herbert arrived back in North Carolina after his "vacation" in Ireland. He did make a side trip to Galway and took the ferry out to the Aran Islands before he flew back home. All his time driving and flying he was thinking of those "black mounds" and the IRA. Could he believe all that? He wasn't entirely convinced.

When he drove up to his office the next morning, he was convinced. It's not often a casket is leaning against your front door. He read the note inside. He looked up and down the street for suspicious activity, but saw none. He didn't even see Desmond parked a block down, laughing at his so-called friend.

Charles and Gina were anxious to get a live report on everything from Herbert. His official version was, "Mark McCarty lived in the Dungloe area for over twenty years, but has recently moved to London with his girlfriend. He is not your ex-husband, Paul." Gina was still skeptical, whereas Charles was happy and relieved. Two million worth of relief. Herbert knew enough to take his pay and keep his mouth shut.

29

BECAUSE OF THE BUSINESS with the private investigator and with the holiday season approaching, Ailin decided, rightly or wrongly, to wait until after the holidays to tell Mark what he had learned about Niamh. If things between them didn't turn out well, he didn't want it to ruin Mark's or Niamh's Christmas. It could wait.

I found myself really missing Thanksgiving, not all the commercialism around it, just the idea of Thanksgiving: family, football, being off work for several days—it was an American tradition. I'm American. Even though the days were much shorter and the rain persisted, the promise of Christmas brought out the cheeriness in nearly everyone. Trees were decorated and store fronts had bright lights and ornaments. I even put up a fake tree in my little apartment, with a few lights and cheap ornaments on it. Mrs. O'Leary even hung a wreath on my door one day and didn't even charge me for it. A true Christmas miracle.

Since the private detective departed everything was back to normal—comfortable, satisfying, and very pleasant.

Even the Amite was somewhat more amicable lately. I could have meals in the restaurant without her causing a scene and giving me indigestion. Ailin had only requested my help one time in December, again to monitor the radio activity. On this trip they drove over to Derry, where again, I sat in the car bored and hungry.

A few days after that trip, Ailin again laid a newspaper on the table, winked at me, and walked away. Inside the national section was an article about all the phone service and internet service outages at the British offices. Apparently, something mysterious had happened at the British Derry headquarters which caused all phone and internet service to be shut down from Friday through Tuesday. Engineers are hard at work repairing the problem and hope to find the cause.

Christmas shopping in Dungloe is difficult. There are not a lot of options. This is why I was happy when Mairead called and asked if I wanted to ride with her to Galway and do some shopping. Galway is a large city, not large like Dublin, but large in a good way. I knew, however, that it was a least a couple of hours away, if not more. I asked Mairead about the distance and she said, quite matter-of-factly, "Oh, we'll spend the night, of course."

Spend the night? What exactly does she mean by that? Together? Certainly not. No way possible. She has to mean she's in one room and I'm in another room. Like friends, or brother and sister. I'm sure that's what she means; however, there is no way I'm going on this trip without telling—no, asking Ailin if it's okay with him.

That evening at our nightly Guinness meeting, I bring it up, shyly saying, "Mairead has asked me to go shopping with her in Galway."

Without looking up from his drink, he replies, "I know. Have fun."

"I think we might spend the night."

I hold my breath now, waiting for his response. Without pause, he says, "Well, you'll have to, it's too far to drive in one day."

Okay, I feel much better now. Ailin knows and doesn't seem to care. Mairead, obviously has informed him of the trip, so that answered a lot of my questions. I know now that it's a simple shopping trip with my friend, nothing more. At least that's what I thought until she pulled up in front of the pub to pick me up and I opened the door. As I started to get in, I could not help but notice the dress Mairead had on. It had a slit up the side of her leg, which was absolutely impossible to ignore. Totally!

She seems all cheery and happy, but I can't decide if I should look her way when talking or keep my gaze straight ahead—away from danger. I know that she knows what she's doing. How could she not? She also knows that I am a male human being, who has not had any female companionship for a long time. She is being either totally unfair or totally suggestive. I have no idea which.

We shop most of the day, stopping only for lunch. Mairead buys a lot of stuff, a lot of expensive stuff. I buy something for Ailin and my landlady, Mrs. O'Leary. I figure I'll give Ruaraidh some sort of alcoholic gift and he'll be thrilled. I still haven't decided if I should search for an Amish gift. Maybe something plain and simple. When Mairead makes a trip to the restroom in her favorite store, I quickly buy her a gift card since I know she loves this place.

She finally finishes with her purchases. My version of shopping is to walk in a store, see something appropriate and buy it. Women are not like that. Women like to shop—which means, try on a lot of stuff but don't buy anything yet. Then they try on other stuff, pick stuff up and hold against themselves, or me, but still don't buy anything. And after much consternation and decision-making, go back to the first thing they saw hours ago and buy it. But with Mairead, it was somehow fun.

She suggests we go to dinner at her favorite spot in Galway, Katharine's. She also says she's already made the hotel booking at a place near the restaurant, within walking distance. But she still doesn't say if she made bookings for ONE room or TWO. Dinner was grand and the wine was expensive. Not good, but expensive. We left the restaurant and after a short walk we arrived at the hotel. Since we were leaving for home in the morning, I wanted to give her the gift card I'd bought so she could use it while we're still here in Galway.

I gave her the gift card in the hotel lobby and she gushed and thanked me with a big hug and a kiss on the cheek. She then said, "I want to give you my gift as well." She had her hands in her coat pocket because it was cold outside. She then brought both hands up and put them around my neck, as if she's going to give me a deep and passionate kiss. But she didn't. Instead, she clasps the necklace she's bought me at the back of my neck and asks me if I "love" it. Well, if Mairead bought it for me, then yes, I do love it.

She booked us separate rooms, both to my disappointment and relief. I slept well, but was subconsciously hoping that the service door connecting our rooms would somehow open during the night and bring me an early Christmas present. It did not. Before I drifted off to sleep I thought of the words to my favorite Irish song, "Galway Girl":

> Well, I took a stroll on the old long walk
>
> I met a little girl and we stopped to talk
>
> And I ask you, friend, what's a fella to do
>
> 'Cause her hair was black and her eyes were blue
>
> And I knew right then I'd be takin' a whirl
>
> 'Round the Salthill Prom with a Galway girl
>
>
> We were halfway there when the rain came down

And she asked me up to her flat downtown

And I ask you, friend, what's a fella to do

'Cause her hair was black and her eyes were blue

So I took her hand and I gave her a whirl

And I lost my heart to a Galway girl

When I woke up I was all alone

With a broken heart and a ticket home

And I ask you now, tell me what you would do

If her hair was black and her eyes were blue

I've traveled around I've been all over this world

Boys I ain't never seen nothing like a Galway girl

We drove home discussing everything from art to music to sports (if you actually consider soccer a sport). She is a joy to talk with as well as a goddess to look at. Just as we're about to arrive in Dungloe, she pulls off the road and stops the car. She says, "I've already told Ailin, and now I want to tell you. After the holidays, if Ruaraidh is okay, I'm moving back to Dublin. We're not getting divorced as of yet. Ailin wants to see what happens. He says he'll visit often and even think of moving. But Mark, even if he does, I'm not sure I want to be married to him.

He wouldn't be happy in Dublin and we'd both be as miserable as I am here."

She doesn't ask for my opinion or advice. She just starts the car and we drive into Dungloe, where she drops me at my apartment and thanks me for a wonderful trip. I still don't know what to say, until she finally looks at me and says sweetly, "I understand."

I meet Ailin for our morning coffee and tea. I started to order some tea, then thought . . . Nah. He did not bring up my trip to Galway with Mairead, so neither did I. We sit mostly in silence, watching a few hopeless souls file in the pub. One guy I'd never seen before came in and ordered a whiskey—straight! Of course, Ruaraidh poured it for him. He downed it and ordered another one. Ruaraidh glanced over at us and Ailin nodded, so Ruaraidh poured him another one. 9:00 in the morning and he's downing shots of whiskey. Ailin looked at me and said, "I think God, in creating man, somewhat overestimated His ability."

Ailin was hurting and I knew it. I also knew there was nothing I could do to help. Tonight was the night of the big Christmas party out at Mairead's house. Ailin had already told me he wasn't going, but Ruaraidh said I could ride with him. I thanked him and half-jokingly asked him if he was going to be sober enough to drive and not get drunk tonight. He looked rather seriously at me and replied, "I only drink to make other people, like you, more interesting."

He and I made it to Mairead's house unscathed, but he was a little "something." I've always heard that being drunk is when you act sophisticated but can't pronounce it. That was Ruaraidh tonight. Everyone in town was at the party. Mairead put on a grand event. She was so busy entertaining it was impossible to say more than hello to her. There were dozens of people floating in and out that I'd never seen before. I figured she had invited people she knew from other villages as well as ours.

Ruaraidh apparently knew everyone and everyone knew him. There was no way I was riding home with him tonight. He stumbled over to me holding a drink in each hand saying, "I want to introduce you to my new friend."

I said, "Okay."

He then turned to his left, then to his right, and said, "Where'd he go?"

I said, "Ruaraidh, please take it easy. You're not gonna know right from wrong if you keep this up."

He smiled and replied, "Yes I will. Wrong is the fun one."

Mairead had a DJ and people danced and laughed and drank. It was fun all around. I simply enjoyed watching everyone. Closer to midnight, the lights were turned down and the music slowed and lovers started their romantic dances. I saw Ruaraidh dancing, or maybe he was just holding on to a rather plump young lady wearing a long dress and boots.

I saw an elderly gentleman, dressed very nicely, ask Mairead to dance. After a minute or two, one of his hands slipped down to Mairead's butt. She discretely moved it back up, then the other hand came down. She backed up a step and said "That's enough, Declan." He smiled a crooked little grin that showed he was missing a couple of front teeth. But I didn't see him grab Mairead's butt again, either.

I'd been sipping the same Guinness for an hour or so when a very attractive young lady that I'd never seen before asked me to dance. Fortunately, it was a slow dance, since I didn't know how to do any other kind. She was very pretty with a fairly short dress showcasing lovely legs and a nice figure. She put her arms around my neck, so I put my arms around her waist, and we danced. It was the best time I'd had in months! She didn't speak and neither did I. I was content holding her and smelling how sexy her perfume was.

When the music stopped, she leaned up and kissed me lightly on the lips, saying "Thank you." I wasn't sure exactly what to do. I didn't know if she was with someone or not, so I tried to follow her through the crowd to keep an eye on her. Then Ruaraidh walked up and blocked my view. I moved to the side, telling him I was trying to keep an eye on a girl I just met.

He said, "Who? Claire?"

"No, not Claire, numbskull. That pretty girl over there in the short dress and nice legs."

"Yeah, Claire."

Have you ever had one of those moments when you are absolutely certain you're in the Twilight Zone?

"No," I repeated, "I'm talking about that pretty girl over there. Not Claire."

He looked over where I was pointing, then looked back at me and said, "Yes, Claire."

I'm bumfuzzled! I say, "Not our Claire, it can't be. It's a different Claire, right?"

"Nope. It's our Claire alright. She's hot! That's why I've been asking her out. How did she kiss?"

"Are you telling me that I just kissed Claire, the Amite?"

He scrunched his face up and said, "What's an Amite?"

"Did I just kiss our Claire from the restaurant?"

"Yep. Are you going to bang her now?"

Fortunately, I didn't hear that last remark. Fortunately, I think I've been beamed into another dimension. There is no way I just kissed the Amite from Hades. Please, Jesus, Mary, and Joseph, tell me it isn't so. I'm still numb when Ruaraidh shakes my arm and says, "She's coming back over here."

I'm still not sure I believe it, however. This woman is pretty. This woman has nice legs. This woman is nice. It can't be Claire. They're playing an awful joke on me. She walks up to me, smiles and says, "I knew you were in love with me," and walks away. Dang, I kissed the Amite! What do I do now?

30

MAIREAD INVITED ME to her house again on Christmas day for lunch with her and Ailin. It was awkward and uncomfortable. Not much conversation, not much of anything. I wanted to leave, but since I rode over with Ailin, I'm stuck. Finally, my luck changes when Ailin says, "Well, I guess we'd better be leaving, unless you want us to help clean up."

Mairead says, "No, I'm sure Mark needs to get back into town." I didn't know what that meant, but it sounded good to me.

Ailin reaches for his coat, then says to me, "So I guess it's true that you and Claire were making out at the party last night."

I stopped buttoning my coat and said, "What? What do you mean, 'making out'?"

Then Mairead chimes in saying, "Well, you did kiss her didn't you?"

"I didn't kiss her! She kissed me and I didn't even know it WAS her."

Ailin slowly nods and says, "It's okay, Mark, she's a pretty girl. Everybody's happy for you."

Mairead smiles— Ailin keeps nodding— I'm trying not to explode.

"Can we just go please?"

On the drive home Ailin asks me if I have plans for New Year's Eve. Honestly, I hadn't even thought about it, but I don't think I can handle another party. Maybe he just wants me to help out at the pub since it's sure to be a big drinking night. Instead, he says, "We'll need your help that night, if you're up to it."

I say, "Sure, anything."

He looks over and says, "We may need you to do a little more than you've been doing. Is that going to be okay?"

Again, I say, "Sure." No more is spoken of it on the drive home. But he doesn't mention Claire either, so I'm happy.

Since the pub was closed Christmas day, people are trying to make up for lost time the day afterwards. We are full and busy all day and night. Ruaraidh was unusually quiet all day. I figured he had a bad hangover. He also had done something to his hair that was unexplainable. I finally asked him if he was okay. He admitted he hadn't been feeling well, but that he probably drank too much yesterday and last night as well. I said, "Well, did you learn a good lesson from that?"

He nodded slightly and said, "Yes, never give yourself a haircut after three margaritas." Then, after a short pause, has asked, "Have you banged her yet?" I looked at him and frowned. That didn't even deserve an answer. Then he said, "Well, have you?"

"Ruaraidh," I said, "I don't know what you drank yesterday to make you so stupid, but it really worked."

Our little group of conspirators left Dungloe around 9:30 on New Year's Eve morning. We did not take the car with all the electronic equipment this time. Instead, we all piled in a nondescript beige colored van. They were all talking to each in heavy Irish accents, with a combination of Gaelic phrases added for emphasis. I really couldn't tell what they were discussing, but I did hear the word Belfast mentioned several times. Belfast, if that's where we are going, is quite far away. It's also the capitol of Northern Ireland and the headquarters of all things British in the country.

Before we left the Republic of Ireland and entered Northern Ireland, we took a side road and met another plain, dark colored van. When we stopped, everyone got out and shook hands; however, they didn't introduce me to anyone. Nor did anyone ask who I was. Then we all started transferring bundles of pamphlets from the dark van over to ours. I couldn't tell what the pamphlets were, except for a picture of an older man on the front.

I had learned a valuable lesson from Ailin: Keep quiet and don't ask questions. After transferring all the bundles we continued our journey into Belfast. I found the city to be rather nice and modern looking. Its history of violence between Catholics and Protestants seemed to be lifetimes away as we wound our way through seemingly normal neighborhoods.

We stopped at a roadside eatery and wasted as much time as possible. We were waiting for darkness, which fortunately came early this time of year. When night came, all the guys put on black coats, black hats, and black gloves. Then they each stuffed as many of the pamphlets into large backpacks as they could fit. Then Ailin gave me my instructions.

I was to drive the van and follow the directions programmed into the GPS system. I would stop at designated areas and each of the guys would get out alone with his backpack. After a quarter of an hour, I was to retrace my route and pick them up one-by-one. Then, we'd go to a different area, where they'd again get out with the pamphlets and I'd pick them up fifteen minutes later. This would continue until all the pamphlets were distributed throughout greater Belfast.

After we'd finished and everyone was safely back in the van, Ailin said, "Let's go home." He took over the driving duties and I sat up front with him, while the others rested in the back for the long ride back to Dungloe. No one spoke much. I think the other guys soon fell asleep. Ailin didn't speak either until we crossed the border back into the Republic. We then stopped for food and drink and they all seemed to ease a bit.

As Ailin and I were drinking a can of Diet Coke and eating fish sandwiches by the van, I asked him what the pamphlets were about. I didn't know if he'd tell me it was none of my business or to shut up, but I asked anyway. He did not hesitate in telling me. I guess he now considered me one of them. He said, "The picture on the front is of the leader of the British consulate in Belfast, probably the most powerful man in the North. On the inside of the pamphlet is unsubstantiated yet credible evidence of a so-called 'love child' he is supposed to have had with a refugee from Botswana. We also have a picture of the child and the mother in the pamphlet.

"We have sources telling us the mother is demanding money from this man and he's paying her to keep quiet. His position of leadership, his reputation, his wife and family could all be jeopardized if this news became public. We just made it public. Our sources told us that he was planning on shipping this 'undocumented refugee' back to Botswana in order to silence her and get rid of her. We made sure that wouldn't happen. He needs to fulfill his obligation to the child and the mother, and hopefully resign his position of leadership. Finally, we're hoping it causes the whole British embassy to say to themselves, 'Those sneaky, devious, contemptible thugs from Ireland are behind this!' We're hoping to give them one more reason to leave our country—one more reason to go home and let Ireland unite again."

※

We arrived back in Dungloe just after midnight and the pub was over-flowing with people. A light snowfall had begun as we each went our separate ways. Ailin retired to his lonely apartment above the pub, probably thinking of all he's lost and wondering if he'll ever regain any of it. The other guys went back to wherever it is they came from: to wives, to girlfriends, to family, or to the loneliness that Ailin lives. Me? I bypassed all the revelry in the pub and walked back to my apartment, tightly gripping a certain pink colored hair clip with little hearts all over it.

31

ON JANUARY 2, after all the partying is done and the village has settled down, Ailin decides he'll tell Mark what he knows about Niamh. That morning he tells those in the pub, "When Mark comes in we are not to be disturbed. Does everyone understand?"

It's an unusually cold morning and I'm looking forward to having a hot cup of coffee in the pub with Ailin. When I walk in, I go directly to the bar and Ruaraidh says, "Boy, are you in trouble." Nothing Ruaraidh says surprises me any longer, so I don't comment. Then Ruaraidh says again, "Ailin's really mad. What did you do?"

"I haven't done anything. What the devil are you talking about?" At that point Ailin sees me and waves me over.

Ruaraidh says, "Good luck buddy, let me know if I can help."

Ailin asks, "What was that about?"

"Oh, I was just arguing with Ruaraidh about something. It was nothing."

Ailin nods and adds, "No matter how smart you are you can never convince someone stupid that they are indeed stupid."

I settle down and let the warm aroma of coffee float through my senses before I actually taste it. I've often thought that the anticipation of that first sip was even better than the actual taste. But maybe not. Usually Ailin stares down at his tea while we sit in silence, but now he's staring directly at me. Maybe I have done something wrong. I ask, "What?"

He takes a small sip of tea, sets his cup down, and says, "I've found her."

I had been thinking to myself that I'd wait for Niamh forever if I had to. Today, forever has lasted only one second. I'm almost afraid to ask who, in case he's NOT referring to Niamh. But I have to.

"Who have you found?"

"Niamh. She doesn't live in Burtonport. She lives near Annagry."

"Annagry? Where is that?"

"Eight miles from Burtonport. Maybe twenty minutes from here."

I have a thousand more questions, but my mind is too confused to ask any of them. Ailin senses my dilemma and volunteers more information.

"My friend knows of her, but he hasn't said anything to her at all. She is NOT married, but she has a young daughter. Her husband was killed in a fishing accident about four years ago. He does not think she's seeing anyone."

As I sat trying to comprehend what I was hearing, he then stunned me even more.

"And, I've met her."

I'm not actually certain if I asked this next question or not. Maybe I wanted to ask it, but couldn't. Maybe I imagined asking it. At any rate he answered it by saying, "I got her address from my friend and drove to her house, under the ruse of asking for directions. First, I wanted to make sure she matched the description of the girl you met and that it was indeed the same Niamh. Second, I'm good at reading people and I wanted to get an impression of her."

Expectantly, I asked, "And?"

"Here's the directions. Take my car and go there now. The rest is up to you. But I'll tell you this my friend . . ." And he was silent for a moment, then continued, "Any man who is fortunate enough to gaze into those emerald eyes, if only for a second, is one of the luckiest men on earth."

On this day after New Year's, Niamh was busy cleaning up her house after her family's visit. Her mother and father left early this morning and her brother was busy getting his things together. He took a break and sat down at the kitchen table to enjoy a cup of tea and a biscuit. His sister was picking up and putting up. Her house was a wreck after her parents and brother spent the last several days playing with and spoiling her daughter.

Niamh finally sat down for a few minutes to talk with her older brother. They missed each other and seldom had time to talk anymore. He eventually asks her if she's seeing anyone, "It's been nearly four years, Niamh. You need to get on with your life."

"Trust me, I want to!" She pours herself a cup of tea and continues, "You should see the type of men asking me out. Drunks, bums, and perverts, each of them wanting to date my insurance money more than me."

He suggests she should move with him to Clifden. "It's a nice town, good schools, and more opportunities for you there. I don't see anything to keep you here now. You'd be closer to Mom and Dad and I could visit my niece more often. Please think about it."

"I will, but I like it here. It's home and I . . ."

"You what?" He asked.

"Probably nothing. But a few weeks ago, Erin's other grandparents had just picked her up in Burtonport and I was finishing a crossword puzzle I'd started."

He stopped her and asked, "Why did they pick her up in Burtonport?"

"It's where we meet—half way between their house and my house. Anyway, I was working on this puzzle waiting for them and wanted to finish it. I hadn't been sitting there more than a couple of minutes when a stranger walked up to my car."

He stopped her again and asked, "A stranger?"

"Yes. I'd never seen him before and he asked me if I'd take him up to that high cliff outside of town. You know it, where the wind blows so hard."

"I remember it," he said, "but why did he ask you to take him up there. And why did he want to go up there in the first place?"

She thought a few seconds, then replied, "I think that he thought I was a taxi driver. He asked me how much it would cost to drive him up there. He was really cute, so I was just playing with him and told him 'four Euro,' and he hopped in my car."

"He just got in your car? And then you drove him up to the cliff?"

She nodded and said, "Yep, that's what happened. Then I kissed him."

"You kissed him?"

"I kissed him. I don't know what came over me. It just seemed like the right thing to do at the time."

Her brother asked, "What did he do?"

"He kissed me back."

"Then what did you do?"

She looked into her tea cup and replied, "Nothing. We stared out into the sea."

"So, you kissed him. Then he kissed you. Then you both stared out into the sea?"

"That's about it. I haven't kissed anyone, nor have I wanted to kiss anyone since my husband died. But something happened that day on the cliff. I can't explain it, but I was hoping it would happen again."

"And you don't know who he was? You let a total stranger get in your car, then you kissed him?"

"I did. And I'd kiss him again if I ever saw him again."

Her brother thought a few seconds, then asked, "And you have no idea if he even lives around here?"

"Oh, I know for sure he doesn't live around here. He's from America. Maybe from Carolina."

"You kissed an American? An American you've never seen before and you don't know anything about him?"

"Yes."

They both sat there and thought about things, her brother being totally flabbergasted by this conversation and Niamh being totally love struck and heartbroken.

Her brother finally thought to ask, "Well, what happened? You kissed him, he kissed you, and that was that? I don't understand. You didn't talk? He didn't ask you out? You didn't ask his name?"

She could only shake her head slowly and say, "It's hard to explain. It was like a magical spell. Then my phone rang and it was Erin calling on her grandparent's mobile phone saying she left her doll in the trunk and they were coming back to meet me. That call broke the spell and I had to rush back into town and meet them. I couldn't think. I didn't know what to do. I didn't know what he thought. It all happened so fast, I was just lost."

"And you haven't seen this American since then?"

"No. I've ridden around Burtonport a few times, but . . . nothing. I've even asked several people if they knew of an American. Again, nothing."

Her brother knew his sister's personal history. He knew she became pregnant after a one-night stand and married in haste, because it was the Catholic way. He knew she and her husband were never in love in the traditional sense. They both did what was expected of them. He knew his sister wasn't happy. He also knew that since her husband's death, she has never met anyone that made her feel like the American did.

They drank a second cup of tea in silence. Her brother didn't know what to say. Neither did Niamh.

32

I TOOK AILIN'S CAR and followed his directions to Annagry. I only took one wrong turn but ended up at the address he'd given me. The address for Niamh. I stopped out front to make sure it was indeed the right place and to practice, for the thousandth time, what I'd say to her. As I started to pull in the driveway, her front door opened and a man carrying a suitcase came out, with Niamh close behind him. He quickly set the bag down, turned around and he and Niamh hugged for several moments.

I didn't move. I watched as they spoke. Then he loaded the suitcase in his car, they hugged again, and he got in the car and started backing out. Then I moved. I have three legitimate choices: I wait for him to leave, then go back and tell Niamh I'm in love with her (am I in love with her)? Second, I keep driving out into the ocean and keep going until I arrive in America. Or three, I go back to Dungloe and give Ailin his car back, then go to the pub, get drunk, pass out, and hope this day never happened.

I turn around and start back to Dungloe, I think. I didn't follow the directions. I didn't pay attention, and I didn't care. At some point during the trip, I pulled the pink hair clip from my pocket and rolled the window down to throw it out; however, a couple of hours later when I arrived back at the pub, I still had the hair clip in my hand. I thought I'd thrown it out. I wanted to throw it out. I intended to throw it out. But, I didn't.

Ailin was inside the pub lecturing the new waitress about something. What? I don't know and I don't care. He asked why I was back so soon and I told him things didn't work out. That was enough. What was I thinking—that a beautiful woman was going to be all alone and waiting for me, like in a fairy tale? He started to reason with me and said, "A word to the wise . . ."

But I interrupted and told him, "Ailin, a word to the wise ain't necessary—it's the stupid ones like me that need the advice."

He wanted more specific information, but I just shook my head and told him Niamh's already involved with someone. End of story. I drew myself a beer since Ruaraidh was out sick again, and went to the corner to sulk and feel sorry for myself, desperately trying to figure out how to eliminate emerald-eyed thoughts from my mind. Reality, it seems, continues to ruin my life.

Winters are not fun in Ireland. It's a damp, windy cold, the sort of weather that blows through your coat right into your bones. Most pubs like ours always a keep fire ongoing in the winter to help people cope with the cold. Usually its peat burning, which doubles not only as warmth, but also fills the room with its aromatic sweetness as well. Sometimes there is a dusting of snow, but more often than not, the temperature is just barely above the snow limit. We get dampness, drizzle, wind, and rain, but seldom snow.

As the cold days linger, there's not much activity in the village. Even Ailin has somewhat curtailed his activities with "the boys." The only perceptible change is Claire's attitude towards me. She has not been rude to me since the ill-fated night of the kiss at the party. In fact, sometimes when no one else is near, she's even nice.

Last night I went into the restaurant for a late dinner. There were only a couple of other customers in there at this hour. The other waitress took my order, but Claire came from the back and walked to my table asking if I needed anything else.

"No. I'm fine, but thanks for asking."

She smiled, which, knowing her, is quite unusual, then asked, "I don't see you around much these days. What are you up to?"

"Oh, nothing much, just work." And trying to be sociable, I returned the question, "And what about you?"

She looked left, then right, then straight back at me and said, "I solemnly swear that I am up to no good whatsoever." Before she walked away she looked at me, but it wasn't a smile or a smirk or a grin. It was like a coquetteish, seducing, Mae West glow. I had to remind myself, Mark, or Paul, this is the Amite you're dealing with here. She's evil, not nice. Yes, she does have nice legs under that tent she's wearing. And yes, she can be attractive when the bun is loose; but still, it's the AMITE!

If my mind could somehow let go of Niamh, I may have seen this encounter differently. But sometimes your heart needs more time to accept what your mind already knows.

In Winston-Salem, Gina and Charles were experiencing the winter of their discontent. After two years of their illicit affair and more than a year of marriage, the glow had gone from their relationship. Or to put in more bluntly, Gina was bored. Her thoughts were consumed with the two million dollars she'd soon be collecting and the life she could then have without the dull, tedious, and tiresome Charles weighing her down. Certainly her newfound riches would enable her to advance in the social circles beyond her reaches now. And she'd probably be able to lure an even more affluent and debonair suiter than the stodgy, work-a-holic Charles.

Indeed, Charles may be a work-a-holic, and a bit stodgy and conservative, and, yes, even boring. But he wasn't stupid. He could see the discontent in Gina's eyes, and especially feel it in the bedroom. He knew from experience what she had done to Paul and he was convinced she was planning his departure as well. After she spent her way through most of his savings, he knew she was looking for new wealth. He knew it was time to visit his old private investigator again.

After the formalities and the small talk ended, Charles said to the investigator point blank, "I'm not asking you to do anything else. I'm not asking you to get yourself in trouble. I'm not asking you to divulge any information or disclose any contacts. But I am asking you to give me a one word answer—that's all. You do that and I'll pay you quite handsomely for the meeting today, and I'll leave and you'll never hear from me again."

Herbert Elkins nodded and replied, "Go ahead. Ask away."

"Are Paul Alfred and Mark McCarty the same person?"

Herbert took a few moments, then said, "I'll give you an answer to your question, but I'll also deny I ever had this conversation with you. And what's more, I'll never agree to see you ever again. Is that understood?"

Charles nodded and said, "I understand."

Herbert then said, "Yes."

Charles rose, turned and walked out the door. They didn't shake hands, nor did they say goodbye. Charles knew what he had to do next. Herbert turned and looked out his window for any suspicious cars or vans that may be carrying wooden coffins.

Charles made the excuse to Gina that he had to go to Minneapolis for a legal convention and would be gone for over a week. Gina was glad to be rid of him. She certainly didn't want to go to Minneapolis in wintertime. Charles reserved his flight, rented his car and booked a hotel for the night in Shannon, Ireland. He was going to find Paul Alfred and offer him a deal he couldn't refuse.

33

CHARLES ARRIVED IN IRELAND with one purpose in mind: find Paul Alfred. He didn't care about sight-seeing or tasting any Guinness or listening to music or anything else. He was a man on a mission. He arrived in Dungloe the following day and did his best to remain as unassuming as possible. He'd brought food with him, so he wouldn't have to eat in any local restaurants. He booked a hotel in a town 30 miles away. Most importantly, he was patient.

He knew what Paul looked like. Even with longer hair and a goatee, he was confident he would recognize him if he saw him. He parked at the end of the main road and sat and observed. After a couple of hours, he drove to the other end of the road and watched. The first day he didn't see anyone he thought might be Paul. The second day he saw someone interesting, but it turned out wrong. The third day, he saw someone enter a pub that matched Paul's height and weight, but he couldn't be sure.

He parked a little closer to the pub and waited. After a few hours Paul Alfred walked out of the bar. He had longer hair and a rather scraggly looking goatee, but it was him alright. Charles was certain. He got out of his car and started walking about thirty yards behind Paul. He followed him to an inn and watched as Paul entered, completely oblivious to his existence.

Charles waited about thirty minutes, just to make sure Paul was staying there, then he went inside. There were stairs and a larger room off to his left with a sign on the door that was marked Manager. Charles knocked on the door. An older woman opened it, but didn't say anything. He thought he'd surprised her, so he spoke quickly saying, "I'm here visiting my friend Mark, but I forgot which room he was in. Can you help me?" She was more than happy to help a friend of Mark's. Charles walked up the stairs and knocked on the door to Mark's apartment.

I had just arrived home and was picking up some of the mess I'd made when there was a knock on my door. There are no peep holes in the old wooden door, but I thought it was probably Mrs. O'Leary. I am shocked when I open it and see Charles standing there. My next reaction is to look down the hallway for Gina. Charles quickly says, "She's not here. She doesn't even know I'm here. No one does, except me and you. Can I come in?"

I step aside and Charles enters, looking around, but keeping his eye on me. Just in case. I do not ask him to sit, nor does he ask me anything. He waits. Charles finally says, "I have an offer for you, and before you turn it down, I want you to think everything through, very carefully."

"The last time I had an 'offer' from you I lost my house, my business, and my wife. I hope you're miserable with her, by the way."

"I am. That's why I'm here. If you don't help me, you'll be miserable, too. Trust me."

"Charles, the last thing on earth I would ever do is trust you."

Charles was expecting this and probably worse. He looks back and says, "Every single thing that has ever happened in your life has been preparing you for this moment—right now. You can decide what you want your future life to be right now. You can continue to be Mark McCarty, or you can be Paul Alfred. It's up to you."

I was skeptical to say the least. I answer, "You're not doing any good deeds for me, Charles. You and Gina gain somehow or you wouldn't be here. It has to be about the life insurance. You're both afraid I'll come back and ruin your two million dollar payday."

Charles smiles and says, "Of course it is. I don't know how you found out about that, but you're right. I won't beat around the bush; here's my offer. Gina is going to leave me probably before she gets the money. The policy is made out to her as the beneficiary. She'll get it all. Unless . . ."

"Okay, I'll bite. Unless what?"

"Unless we make a deal with her—you and me."

"What sort of deal? And why would I want to deal with a snake like you, Charles?"

Charles then began to lay out his scheme. "Gina wants the money. I want some of it to restore what she's spent of my savings. And you want to be left alone. Is that correct?"

I reply, "I know Gina always wants money. I could care less if you restore anything or not. But I do want to be left alone."

"You and I can both get what we want and hurt her in the process."

"What's your plan?"

"I take a few pictures of us together to prove you are still alive and we're teaming against her. When she sees the pictures, all that money will evaporate right before her eyes. Then I tell her how she can still benefit—not quite as much, but she'll still come out way ahead and be rid of me in the process."

"Keep going." I say.

"I'll tell her that unless she agrees to everything, you'll come back and she'll get nothing. Plus, she and I will be prosecuted for insurance fraud as well and probably end up in jail."

"Good! I hope you both end up in jail."

"But if we go to jail, so will you my friend—skipping out on debts, illegally leaving the country, false identity, and who knows what else they'll come up with. No, my plan is the only thing that makes sense for all of us."

Disgustedly, I ask him to tell me the rest of his plan.

"I tell Gina that she can have $1 million of the insurance money. I'll take $500,000 and you can have the other $500,000 if you agree not to expose us for the insurance scam. If any one of us doesn't agree, we all lose. If we do agree, then she is still a millionaire. I get some of my money back that she spent. And you get a nice nest egg and we don't expose you. Win-win-win!"

I know Charles and I don't trust him. "How will I know that you two will keep your word and never expose me?"

"Because, if we expose you, then it also exposes us—insurance fraud! We all go to jail."

It's really a pretty easy decision for me, so I tell Charles, "Go ahead with your plan; however, I don't want any of your illegal money. Give her whatever you want and keep whatever you want. But leave me out of it and leave me alone. I don't want to ever hear from either of you ever again. Agreed?"

This was indeed a bonus for Charles. Now he doesn't have to split his share, he gets it all. He sticks his hand out towards me to shake on the deal, as he says, "Agreed."

When Charles offers his hand for me to shake on the deal, I tell him to get out of my apartment, get out of Dungloe, and get out of Ireland. As Charles is merrily skipping down the steps, I call to him and say, "And Charles, if I ever see you again, I'll beat you to a pulp."

I'm pretty sure I'll never see or hear from either Charles or Gina again. I'm also sure that Dungloe is now my home forever. There's no going back.

34

I WATCH CHARLES walk down the street, get in his car, and drive away. Then I go to the pub and wait for Ailin. I have to talk to someone. But as soon as I walk in, I'm put to work. Ruaraidh has gone home sick again. We're going to have to do something about all his absences. When Ailin arrives, I motion for him to come to the end of the bar where we can talk in relative privacy.

I first let him know about Ruaraidh and he tells me he'll have a serious talk with him. Then I tell him about Charles and my visit today. Surprisingly, he says, "I've been waiting for that."

Shocked, I answer, "You've been waiting for Charles? You knew he was coming?"

"No. Not that. I've been waiting to hear you say that Dungloe is now your home forever. Now that you've said it, I have a proposition for you."

"What?"

"I have an associate in Donegal—that's all you need to know—who 'helps' me with certain paperwork issues. I've talked to him and he can arrange you proper identification. He'll give you a birth certificate—you were orphaned by the way—and prepare a passport and any other documentation you might need to become a full-fledged Irishman. Everything except an accent; you'll have to work on that yourself. What do you say?"

What DO I say? I'm an American. I'm proud to be an American. I'll always be an American, but I'm no longer Paul Alfred and I never will be again. I'm Mark McCarty now, and I guess I always will be. So, even though I'll always be an American, I will now also be an official Irishman as well.

"Thanks, Ailin. What do I need to do?" And with that conversation, I became Irish. Ailin brought me my paperwork in a few days and it was done.

I joined in a few missions with Ailin and the boys, always as the driver and radio monitor. One adventure, I found out later, was to simply get into the local newspaper office in Londonderry. Somehow they managed to change the picture on the front page of the British Prime Minister with that of James Bond. Anything they could do to get under the skin of the Brits.

Other than that, most of the winter days were ordinary and uneventful. Mairead came into the pub several times and we had nice conversations, but I could tell something was going on with her. I had several very weird conversations with Claire. She called one day and asked me if I could come over. Usually, she would "tell" me to come over, so I knew something was up.

When I arrived, the plump waitress told me Claire was in the back and to go meet her there. When I walked in the kitchen area, no one else was there except the Amite. She looked at me and said, "Oh, what are you doing here?"

"You asked me to come here. Is everything okay?"

"Oh, yes. Everything is fine. I was only wondering if YOU needed help with anything? Anything at all?"

As I'm trying to understand exactly what she's talking about, she walks over right in front of me and says, "If you do need help with anything, just let me know. Okay?" Then she brushes up against my arm as she walks out of the kitchen. As I'm contemplating this occurrence, I remember a saying from my days growing up in rural North Carolina, "When women go wrong, men go right after them." Was Claire going wrong? Am I going after her? No way!

Later that evening I tell Ailin about this encounter with Claire and he just laughs and says, "I told you she's in love with you."

"Ailin, you are crazy!"

He looked seriously at me and replied, "Mark, when was the last time you did something for the first time?" As I'm trying to understand exactly what he means, he continues, "When you stop doing things for fun, you might as well be dead." He then stood up, patted me on the shoulder, and went upstairs.

The next morning Ruaraidh calls in sick again. Or is he just hung over? Either way, we need to address all these continuing absences. When Ailin comes down, he tells me he'll ride out to see Mairead and see if she knows what's going on with Ruaraidh.

Instead of being gone all day, Ailin arrives back at the pub before noon. He walks in and motions for me to follow him. We go to the back corner and sit down. He waves the waitress away. This must be serious if he doesn't want tea or Guinness. He's as serious as I've ever seen him. He takes a deep breath and tells me Ruaraidh is dying.

I don't know what to say. I don't know what to ask. How? Why? What? It doesn't make sense.

He starts to explain, "Mairead told me Ruaraidh has been sick for quite a long time. His liver is very bad. In fact, it's beyond repair. If he'd followed doctor's orders and stopped drinking and done what they've been telling him to do for the past year, he might've been okay. But he didn't. He kept drinking. He wouldn't take the medicines and he quit going for the treatments. The cirrhosis has developed to the point of being inoperable and untreatable. He's going to die."

I am completely shell-shocked. None of us had any idea, including Ailin. I finally recover to ask, "How long does he have? Can't we take him to Dublin or London and have a specialist take a look at him?"

Ailin says, "Mairead took him to Galway three weeks ago for second opinions. They all agreed. He's waited too long and neglected himself too much. Maybe two months. Maybe less. He's going to stay with Mairead until he needs the hospital."

Needless to say, when the news of Ruaraidh spread around town, a dark gloom set in. Everyone wanted to visit him, but Ruaraidh requested no visitors. He wanted to be alone. Ailin is the only person allowed to see him and he reports Ruaraidh is not well at all. He's losing weight and has no energy whatsoever.

The music still played in the pub. Guinness was served and conversations were held, but no one enjoyed any of it. Early the following week, I received a phone call from Mairead. Could I come out and visit? Of course. Ruaraidh looked yellowish, tired, and in a lot of pain. He was sitting up, but it wasn't easy for him. When I walked in the room he looked at me and said, "Mark, bring me a beer!"

We all talked and laughed and told stories, mostly of the funny things Ruaraidh had done when he was drinking. He told me he was ready to go; he was tired of the pain. Then, he asked me the question I'd been asked out here for. "Will you take me to the cliffs?"

"Take you to what cliffs? What does that mean?" I truly had no idea what he meant.

He said, "The Cliffs of Moher, eejit. I saw them as a lad and I want to see them again before I'm gone. Will you do it?"

If you have the power to make someone happy, do it! The world needs more of that. Of course I would. At the time I had no idea what these cliffs were or where they were, but if my friend wanted to see them, then see them he would. His eyes glistened and he said, "I knew you wouldn't let a good friend down."

I looked back at him and replied, "Ruaraidh, when you're in jail, a good friend will be there trying to bail you out. A best friend will be in the cell next to you saying, 'Dang, that was fun!' That's us—best friends."

35

SPRING WAS STILL several weeks away, so I knew the tourists wouldn't be all that bad where we were going. I'd learned that the Cliffs of Moher were 800 foot high, starkly vertical cliffs on the west coast below Galway. Once Ruaraidh, or anyone, had seen them, you could never forget them because they were extremely photogenic and breathtaking. Mairead lent us her car so we could leave early Saturday morning on our adventure.

I left the pub fairly early Friday evening to pack and prepare for the trip. I was shirtless in my apartment, trying to find some clean underwear when I heard a knock on the door. I was hoping Charles, or worse yet, Gina, was not out there looking for me. It was worse yet. It was the Amite.

I opened the door and without asking if she could enter, Claire walked right in. Or, I should say, she vamped right in. Her hair was down, her dress was short, and she smelled of alcohol. She was not trying to hide her intentions in the least. She said, "I thought you might enjoy some company."

"Claire, tonight's not really a good night for me. I'm sort of busy."

"What?"

When a woman says 'What?' it's not because she didn't hear you. She's giving you a chance to change what you said. I rephrased my comments, "Claire, I'm going on a trip and I need to pack and take care of some things. I hope you understand." She didn't.

She did not like this statement either. Not at all. Her mood suddenly changed from vixen to she-devil, and she said, "Why don't you put a shirt on? You look fat!"

This is the Claire I know. I responded, "I'm happy that I'm fat. Otherwise, I'm pretty sure I'd be an absolute slut."

"Are you calling me a slut?"

"No, I'm not, Claire. I'm telling you I don't have time for anything tonight. Not you, or anyone else." I then quickly filled her in on my trip with Ruaraidh in the morning and she seemed to soften a bit. Then, incredibly enough, Claire, the Amite from Hades, began to cry. I didn't know what to do.

She said, "I got all dressed up and thought you might like me. After all, you did kiss me."

"Claire, it's not that I don't like you (I lied). It's just that I'm busy tonight and I need to help Ruaraidh. And, to tell you the complete truth, I like someone else. I REALLY like someone else."

"Who?"

"Someone you don't know. She's not from around here. She's someone who doesn't even like me back. She's someone who's involved with another person. But I can't help feeling the way I do. Can you understand?"

She started to cry more and I asked if she was okay. She whimpered, "I just want someone to look at me like I look at chocolate cake."

As weird as that sounded, I know what she means. Trying to reassure her—and get her to leave— I said, "Claire, you're a beautiful woman. Any man would be lucky to have you."

She said, "I know that. But I don't know what to do. All the men around here are such fools. I've tried everything."

Okay, here goes nothing. "Well, have you tried dressing a little less business-like at work? Not like you're dressed now, but maybe a combination of the two. And let your hair down as well."

She instantly stopped crying and said, "Really?"

"Yes." I said, "Let people see the real you. I guarantee men will be lined up outside the restaurant."

She thought about this for a few seconds, then quickly turned and walked to the door. She then looked back over her shoulder at me and said, "Thanks."

Mairead helped me get Ruaraidh into the car Saturday morning. He was in a lot of pain and not good. We drove south, bypassing Galway and finding a nice B&B near Kinvarra. Ruaraidh slept most of the way and all of the evening and night as well. At those infrequent times he did wake, he kept taking some sort of pill, for pain I imagine. We rose early Sunday morning and I had a nice, full Irish breakfast. Ruaraidh couldn't eat anything. He only had tea.

We drove to the parking area near the cliffs and I left him in the car while I went and rented a wheelchair for him. He was groggy and almost incoherent until we reached the edges of the cliffs. Then, the wind, the sea mist, and the general excitement brought him fully awake. I rolled him up and down the walkway while we both stared in awe and wonder. We were 700-800 feet straight up from the sea with spectacular vistas up and down the coastline.

Ruaraidh was overcome. He started crying a little, remembering the scenes from his visit years ago with his mom and dad. Then his emotions completely took over. Certainly, we looked quite the pair to the other tourists, a man pushing another man in a wheelchair who was crying. When he gained control, he looked up at me and said, as he was pointing out to sea, "You're from across the ocean, aren't you?"

"Not anymore, Ruaraidh. I'm from here." We stayed until he couldn't hold his head up any longer. We found a nice spot off the walkway and sat admiring the view, each of us contemplating our own journey in life. We drove back to the same B&B in Kinvarra and I put him to bed. He slept through the evening and night; I thought of emerald eyes and grasped a pink hair clip. Monday morning I could barely get him into the car. He slept all the way back to Dungloe. Mairead met us in the driveway and immediately started crying. She knew. We all knew.

My friend Ruaraidh died appropriately and fittingly on March 17, St. Patrick's Day. It was a grand occasion and, as he would have wanted, we all raised several glasses to our friend, our mate, our brother. Everyone in Dungloe was at the funeral. Good people bring out the good in people. The priest made everyone cry and then made everyone think. He said, "Faith in God includes faith in his timing. And the one lesson we should all learn from Ruaraidh is that we should enjoy life now. This is not a rehearsal."

That evening, after the funeral, after nearly everyone had left the pub, Ailin waved me over to his table. He was drinking an Irish whiskey. He looked up from his glass and said, "Mairead is moving to Dublin as soon as she can arrange everything."

I know full well a response from me is not needed. But my presence is. We sit in silence as he slowly sips his whiskey and I drink my Guinness. We closed the bar, but we didn't leave. We sat in silence and in solitude reflecting on the loss of our friend and the loss of a wife.

36

AILIN WASN'T HIMSELF. He stopped leaving us all day, and instead, he hung around the bar. He even told me to take off one day, he would take care of things. What does a displaced American/new Irishman do on a cold Wednesday morning? I firmly clutched my pink hair clip and went to the bus station. Yes, I still have it. No, I can't throw it away. I just don't want to live the same year 75 times and call it a life.

I took the bus to Burtonport first. I walked around the town a bit, then made my way to the pub. The older bartender from before recognized me and came over. He asked, "Did you ever find that taxi you were looking for?"

I smiled at him and replied, "Yep, I found it alright. It left me and went out of business."

"So, what are you doing over here in our fair village today?"

After some reflection, I said, "Sir, I don't know. Lately, I seldom seem to know what I'm doing."

He nodded and smiled a bit, then replied, "Don't worry, Sonny. No one else knows what they're doing either."

I left the pub and walked around to the corner where the "For Hire" sign was. I sat on the bench and reminisced about a taxi ride I'd taken with the most beautiful set of emerald eyes this side of Tir-na-nOg. After a suitable time of reflection, I went back to the bus station. But instead of taking the bus back to Dungloe, I took the next bus to Annagry. In life, if you don't risk anything, you risk everything.

I had no intention of going out to Niamh's house, even if I could have remembered the way. I only wanted to . . . I don't know what I wanted. I guess I just wanted to be near her. I walked along the streets and met the stares from the locals wondering who the devil I was. I sat in the only pub in town and had a plain. I dreamed. I wished. I prayed. But reality kept rearing its ugly head and reminding me that the truth will always be the truth, even if I never believe it.

I caught the bus back to Burtonport, and learned that the next bus to Dungloe wasn't until 8:00 tonight. My options, being extremely limited, forced me back to the local pub until the bus came. Since I would be there a couple of hours, I took a table in the back and ordered dinner and a drink. As in nearly every pub in Ireland, people started filtering in and roaming about. Some came to drink, some to have a sandwich, some just to mingle and listen to the nightly music. I could do all three.

Just like in our pub, eventually people started stirring and musicians started playing. The difference here was that all the musicians were women. They sat in a circle facing each other. There were two women with guitars, one older and one teenaged, and one middle aged-woman who played a tambourine and the harmonica. Two more women played violins, or fiddles, as the case may be.

I was thoroughly enjoying the entertainment and figured I had time for one more Guinness before catching the bus. I wound my way from the back of the pub up to the bar and ordered my drink. As the bartender was allowing it to "cook," I looked over toward the band directly at the woman facing away from me. I was shocked to see a pink hair clip, with little hearts all over it, holding back a lock of light brown hair, with just a slight tinge of red. The woman with the hair clip was playing her fiddle as hard as she could. The bartender gave me the drink and others were behind me, so I had to move.

As I weaved my way back, it was difficult to look at the band. I was afraid I'd trip or bump into someone. From my table, the woman with the hair clip was still facing away from me. I couldn't tell if it was Niamh or not. Think, Mark! I notice the restroom at the far end. I start that way, trying to look at the fiddle player, while not tripping over something or someone. There's an open space just before the bathroom so I stop and turn around. It is Niamh. Her beautiful green eyes are closed as she's playing the most soulful melody I've ever heard. She is even more gorgeous than I'd remembered.

I went into the bathroom, washed my face and quickly came back out. I looked around for the man I'd seen her embracing that day in front of her house, but I didn't see him. The band was still playing and her eyes were still closed. I went back to my little table trying to convince myself, with every excuse known to man, that I should go and speak to her. I failed. I sat and listened and looked. Knowing those emerald eyes, and pink hair clip with the little hearts, would be leaving the pub tonight with someone other than me.

I couldn't take my eyes off her. I was totally transfixed when someone asked me if they could use the other chair at my table. Sure. That's when I looked at my watch and saw it was 8:45. I quickly made my way outside to the bus stop. Too late. No more buses to Dungloe tonight. No taxis either. 10 miles doesn't seem that far, unless you have to walk it. No problem. The thoughts of green eyes and light brown hair made it seem as though I was walking on air. I made it back to my apartment at 11:55. Even after walking for over three hours, I still could not sleep. But I could dream.

I returned to the pub in Burtonport three out of the next four nights. No Niamh. The bartender said the group of women playing that night only play from time to time— no set schedule. Why am I chasing her? What would I do if I even saw her again? What am I doing with my life? Why am I chasing a dream? Well, Mark, old boy, I tell myself, you can live your life or repent not having lived it.

Ailin doesn't meet me for our tea and coffee this morning. Maybe he's off with "his boys," or maybe he's just off. I don't know. But I do take advantage of his absence and go to the restaurant for a good breakfast. It's been several days since I've been in and I am shocked at what I see. Claire, the she-devil, potato-sack wearing, plain-Jane Amite has transformed herself. She has on a short skirt, with a tight blouse, exposing a rather voluptuous figure. Instead of a bun on top of her head, her hair is flowing and accentuated with sparkling earrings. And she's smiling. Well, not at me, but she's smiling.

For the first time ever, I'm disappointed not to have her take my order. Instead, I get the plump girl who is just plump—not pregnant. Claire flits and flirts around, obviously enjoying the attention her new wardrobe and makeover have allowed her. She avoids me completely. I ask for second and third cups of coffee hoping to have a word with her, but she stays away. As I rise to leave, she comes out of the kitchen, looks my way, and says in a loud enough voice for everyone to hear, "You can keep asking, but I seriously doubt I'll ever date you." But instead of scowling, she winks at me and returns to the kitchen.

All Ailin's businesses seem to be doing well now. Is it a coincidence that they're making a profit since I started helping? I don't know, but it makes me feel good. I'm anxious to discuss this with Ailin tonight when he returns. I'm secretly hoping for a nice compliment and pat on the back. He comes into the pub a little after dark and doesn't speak to anyone as he goes over to his usual table. Our new bartender who we hired to replace Ruaraidh brings him a Guinness and leaves without a word. He's learned well.

I wait for Ailin to settle and he looks over at me and nods—which means, "come on over." As usual, I wait for him to start any conversations we might have. He finally asks if everything is okay. I'm not entirely sure if he's asking is everything okay with me personally or is everything okay with the business. But I'm excited to tell him of the business part, so that's what I start with. I review each one and document all the good news for him. He keeps nodding while taking it all in. When I finish, he looks up at me and says, "Good job. But never let success go to your head. And never let failure go to your heart."

Again, I'm quite certain that silence is indeed the best response at this moment. He changes the subject and asks me again if there's anything new with Niamh. I answer, "Ailin, I've learned that to ignore the facts does not change the facts. She's involved with someone else and that's that. I just accept it and try to move on." I say this to him as I'm holding on tight to the hair clip in my pocket. I'm such a liar.

He looks directly at me for several seconds, in fact, so long I have to look away. Then he says, "I'm going to Dublin."

"Okay," I answer. "When will you be back?"

"I'm not coming back. I'm going there to win back Mairead, as long as it takes. You're now in charge." If I'd seen old Mrs. O'Leary doing a pole dance on Main Street, I wouldn't have been more surprised. He continued, "I can't go back in time and change things and start a new beginning. But I can start today and make a new ending."

My mind is buzzing uncontrollably. Is my life here in Dungloe over? How will the town survive without Ailin? What happens with the IRA boys? Where do I go now? While I'm still trying to digest this bombshell of information, he says, "Mark," shaking me back to reality, "you're in charge of everything now."

"I'm in charge of everything? What does that mean?"

"It means you are in charge of everything! All the businesses, all the finances, the pub, the responsibilities, the decisions and 'the boys.' You can handle it." I look at him dumbfounded. He looks at me and says, "Close your mouth. I've already handled all the financial stuff at the banks and all the accounts. Your signatures are as good as mine everywhere I do business. I'll leave you my number and you can check with me anytime, though I'd prefer you didn't. I trust you. All the businesses are doing well, they are all making money, and you are the main reason for that. Any questions?"

"Are you kidding me? I have about a thousand questions."

He says, "You'll be fine. Just keep doing what you've been doing."

I ask him, "Are you sure about this Ailin? I mean really sure?" Of course, I'm referring to me and businesses.

He answers, "Absolutely. I can't live without her. I'll do whatever it takes and be the man she wants me to be. I'll adjust to Dublin. I'll adjust to anything to get Mairead back."

I feel for him. I only now realize how much he's hurting. I say, "Okay. Go to her. Be all that she wants you to be. Don't worry about this, we'll be fine. But, there is one thing I want to clarify."

He looks at me and says, "I know. The boys."

"Ailin, I have no idea what you and the boys do. I'm not one of them. They'll never accept me. Can't Turlough handle that and I'll help out when needed?"

"I thought about that. But Turlough is incapable of making decisions. The other two have good ideas, but they need someone with a good mind to organize things and decide what's good and what's not good. You'll have to make sure they don't do crazy stuff and NEVER hurt anyone. Other than that, do the best you can to make life miserable for the Brits. And, Mark, this is important. Don't get caught."

We sat in silence for a few moments and then he said, "I'm leaving in the morning. I want you to move into the apartment upstairs. It's fully furnished and it's yours now. I won't be back." He didn't give me a chance to say anything before he rose and walked away, up the stairs for the last time.

37

SPRING IS JUST AROUND the corner in our part of the world. The daily rains will be less frequent, flowers will blossom, and everything will turn at least thirty-six different shades of green. People will get outside more often and little kids will be running down the streets. The sun will make everyone smile and sheep will be gorging on all the new growth. While everywhere else in Ireland, the tourists will temporarily take over. The Blarney Stone will be kissed ten thousand times and the little town of Dingle will be overrun with young people wishing and acting like they were flower children from the sixties. The Rock of Cashel will impress everyone, and the Guinness Brewery tour will make everyone happy. The little, thatch-roofed town of Adare will certainly recall days of old and Dublin will impress with its elegance and urbanity. While life here in Dungloe continues to roll onward like the River Shannon to the sea; oblivious to the hubbub of tourism and modernity. Just the way we like it.

When news spread that Ailin was gone, it was like total shock had set in. It took several days for things to get back to normal. Mrs. O'Leary wasn't very happy I was moving out of the apartment. She wasn't sad to see ME leave; she was upset about losing the rent. But I was happy. Ailin's apartment over the pub was a vast improvement over my tiny apartment at Mrs. O'Leary's. I could entertain any young ladies there and be proud of my home. Who am I kidding? What young ladies? I really need to throw this hair clip away. Maybe tomorrow.

One of the perks of my new responsibilities was I got to drive one of the cars Ailin used for his adventures with the boys. It was the car with all the electronic equipment in front. But I didn't care. It would still get me over to Burtonport hopefully to listen to an all-girl band play.

I had my first meeting with "the boys." I was the referee. They would come up with ideas and then argue what to do, when to do it, and who would do what. Ailin was right about one thing. Turlough wouldn't say anything or give an opinion, but he would do whatever I asked him to. After much bickering, I would decide which one of the projects we should do next. After I made the decision, all of them would be happy. Apparently, whatever Ailin told them about me seemed to work.

One of the two younger guys was a complete technological junkie. He had hacked into several branches of the British government in Belfast and monitored their correspondences. We decided our next project would be to copy some of the more "personal and sexually explicit" emails being sent out. It seems as though quite a few of these mid-level officials had extra time on their hands and were emailing girlfriends, boyfriends, and in some cases, each other's wives.

We thought it would be appropriate to share these emails with everyone. And I do mean everyone. My two partners had email mail lists of tens of thousands of people throughout Northern Ireland. These leaked emails would greatly embarrass quite a few of the Brits. That was our intention.

Again, they argued over which emails to send out and how many to send out. After I made a decision, it was then settled, no further arguments. It was very interesting to monitor all the different papers in the following days to see the reactions from our handiwork. I'm sure each and every British official was cursing us and wishing they were back home in England. So were we.

Now that I had my own transportation, I made the trip over to Burtonport more often. But I never saw an all-girl band playing. One afternoon I even made the short trip over to Annagry. I am not a stalker. I am not a pervert. All I did was ride by her house. All I did was clutch a certain pink colored hair clip with little hearts all over it and dream of an afternoon on a windy cliff.

One evening at the pub in Burtonport, as I was ordering a drink, the bartender said, "You must really like the music here."

"Yes, I do."

"But…." He said, looking at me waiting for an answer.

"But what?"

"But why is an American, living in Dungloe, coming to my little pub, in the middle of nowhere, several times a week?"

Not knowing what to say, I just shrugged.

He smiled and said, "They'll be back here Saturday night."

I looked back at him and asked, "Who will be here Saturday night?"

"Who you've been looking for week after week. That's who."

I'm at a loss. How does he know? I don't know what I should or should not say.

"Sonny . . . it's Mark, right? We're a small town and we all notice a stranger around. Especially when that stranger is an American. I saw you stumbling around the bar staring at the girls that night they were playing. It's one of them you're interested in isn't it?"

No use lying about it now. "Yes, I'm sorry. I didn't mean to be that obvious or make anyone uncomfortable. Especially anyone in the band."

"No worry. No one has brought anything up. But it's my job to notice things—to see if anyone has had too much to drink or needs to go home. I noticed you. But I'm certain the band didn't. Which one are you interested in?"

248

"One of the fiddle players, but please don't say anything to her. I wouldn't want that."

He smiled and said, "Oh, I won't say a word. None of my business and I want them to keep coming back. They play for drinks, which is good for me because it brings in customers—like you."

I nod at him and ask, "Saturday night, you say?"

"Be here about half nine."

Niamh answered her phone and was surprised to hear her brother's voice. He was thinking of coming to visit her again. "Well," she said, "my group is playing at a pub in Burtonport Saturday night. Why don't you come and meet up with me there. Then you can listen to us and tell me what you think of our music."

They talked about Niamh's daughter and their parents and then her brother once again brought up the idea of her moving to Clifden, near him. She was non-committal. She liked her musician friends and her daughter was just starting school in Annagry. But her social life in the tiny village was indeed stifling. She told him she was still thinking about it. What she didn't tell him was that she was also still thinking about a kiss, high on a cliff, on a windy day, not long ago.

Niamh and her group arrived early at the pub in Burtonport to get set up. They enjoyed playing in public, it gave them the opportunity to practice before a live audience. They could enhance their skills while getting a good idea if people really liked their music. Their goal was to someday be good enough to make their own CD. Niamh's brother met them before the music started and sat at a small table up front near the band of women.

38

THURSDAY AND FRIDAY were interminable. Turlough called me Friday morning to ask what I was up to. Instead of answering him, I asked him the question I'd been wondering about since my first day in Dungloe: "Turlough, what did you and the boys do with Ailin every day?"

After a moment of silence he said, "What do you mean? We didn't do anything with Ailin every day. He'd call us occasionally and we'd meet and try to decide what we needed to do, if you know what I mean."

Totally perplexed, I said, "But he was away from Dungloe all day, every day. I thought he was meeting with you and the boys."

"Oh, no, we have to work. We all have jobs. We couldn't meet with Ailin. We'd only see him when we came up with an idea that we wanted to run past him."

I asked, "Well, what did do every day, if he wasn't meeting with you?"

"He was writing. He'd take his laptop and go off to a lake, or a stream, or maybe the ocean, and sit and write. He said it gave him inspiration and he enjoyed the solitude."

Well, another mystery solved. I wish the emerald-eyed mystery was this easy to solve. At least I'll get to see her again Saturday. And then I wonder should I even go. Why keep torturing myself? And why do I always find myself with my hand in my pocket holding onto this darned hair clip?

Saturday morning I make my way to the restaurant for breakfast. I've come to really enjoy my bacon, ham, sausage, eggs, and baked beans, but I'll never like the tomatoes— I'm not that much of an Irishman yet. As I take a seat I notice Claire at the cash register and I nod to her. She doesn't notice because there are several young men floating around her, some paying their bills, others waiting to be seated, I assume. I don't really know.

Then Claire walks from behind the counter and I see why the young men are all milling about. She has on the shortest miniskirt this side of Haight-Ashbury in the late '60's! She wobbles over to my table, apparently having trouble adjusting to the stylish high heels she's also wearing, and whispers, "My feet are killing me."

"Well, take off those shoes and put on something more comfortable."

"Oh, I can't do that."

I ask why not and she says, "Because of them." Pointing to all the men staring at her, she tells me the restaurant's business has been booming lately. Apparently, young men really enjoy eating in a restaurant with short skirts and long legs. And after all these years of Amish, long dresses, Claire is loving the attention.

I enjoyed a second cup of coffee, served by the plump waitress—Claire was busy with the other guys. I get up to leave and from across the room, she says, "When I say no, I mean NO!" I start to say something wise back to her, but instead, she just smiles at me and I leave.

I fiddle about the bar, getting in everyone's way. I then go up to the apartment and read a book Ailin wrote about Irish history. I take a shower and change clothes and it's still only 7:00. A long time till half nine. I start reading again and after the chapter on Oliver Cromwell, the phone rings.

"Hello."

"Mark, I'm so glad you answered." It's Mairead and she sounds frantic.

"Mairead, are you alright?

"Yes, I'm fine. It's Ailin I'm worried about.

"Worried? What's wrong? Is he hurt, or sick?"

"No, he's fine physically, but emotionally he's a wreck. I'm afraid he's going to do something stupid."

This is not good. I know it's not good. And I know I shouldn't ask this next question, but I have to. "It's about you and him, isn't it?"

"Mark, there is no me and him. I came to Dublin to get away from him. I've realized I can't be with him again. Ever. But he doesn't understand that and won't take no for an answer. He's following me everywhere I go."

"What's he doing when he follows you?"

She seems to be crying a little as she answers, "Nothing. He just follows me, to concerts, when I go out to eat with friends, to the university. Lord knows if he was ever to see me with another man, I don't know what he'd do."

I don't know what to say. They're both my friends. So I wait for her.

"You have to help me Mark."

Oh no, this is what I was afraid of. "Help you do what, Mairead? What can I do?"

"You have to talk to him. Convince him to leave me alone and get on with his life. He trusts you. He'd listen to you. You have to help me Mark. You have to help us both."

Jesus, Mary, and Joseph . . . what have I gotten myself into?

"Okay, I'll call him tomorrow."

"No! You have to come to Dublin and see him face-to-face. You're going to have to sit down with him and convince him to go back to Dungloe and get on with his life. That's the only way. Will you do it? Will you come here to Dublin, Mark? Please?"

What can I say? "Yes, I'll come. But I don't know that he'll listen to anything I say, Mairead. You know how strong-willed he is."

"You just come and try. I'm going to call Aer Lingus and make you a reservation from Galway to Dublin tomorrow. What time can you be in Galway tomorrow?"

I tell her the afternoon would be best, and we say our goodbyes. This is not good. I ask myself what kind of king-sized mess have I gotten mixed up in. I'm so dismayed at this entire episode that I don't realize it's nearly 9:00.

39

FORTUNATELY, Burtonport is only a short drive away. But by the time I get to the pub on this Saturday night, it's packed. There are no tables available so I find an empty spot at the bar next to an old, old man. He turns and speaks to me, but I have absolutely no idea what he's saying. I smile back at him and he laughs and pats me on the knee. The bartender recognizes me and says, "They'll be right out."

I don't know why I'm excited, but I am. I don't know exactly what I think I'm doing here—but I'm here. I didn't know I was this crazy, but apparently, I am. I grasp the hair clip in my pocket a little tighter and convince myself it's all very innocent. I tell myself there's no way on God's green, Irish earth I would ever actually talk to Niamh tonight. And I know I'm lying.

I drink my first Guinness so fast that I have to consciously tell myself to "slow down." The old man next to me turns again to face me and then leans in close to say something which, again I absolutely don't understand. His accent and his breath are so bad it's impossible for me to even fake that I understand him. But he doesn't seem to care—he just laughs again and pats me on the knee.

Before my second Guinness arrives, the girls in the band start filtering in. One by one they arrange their chairs in the front of the pub and take their instruments out of the cases. Niamh is not facing me, but her back isn't to me either. I can see the side of her face and when she turns to talk to the other girls, I can see her fully. From this distance I can't really see how beautiful those emerald eyes are . . . but I know they are.

Soon, they start playing and I'm transfixed. The old man next to me is in my sightline a little, so I have to keep twisting and turning to see well. I have no plan whatsoever. I keep debating one of two options for myself. One, I just wait for a break in the music, walk up to them, and speak to her, hoping she'll remember me. (And hoping her boyfriend isn't here and doesn't try to punch me in the nose.) Or, the second option, I wait for a break in the music and casually walk past her, hoping SHE'LL recognize me!

They play solidly for over an hour before they take their first break. Someone from the bar brings them drinks and they sit and talk amongst themselves while relaxing. I still can't decide which option would work best, but I think actually trying to talk with her might be hard. There's so many people around her and she's constantly talking to the other girls in between songs.

As I start my third Guinness, I decide that at the next break in the music, I'll casually weave my way through the crowd and walk directly in front of her—not looking at her of course, just being aloof and debonair. Three pints of Guinness makes you think like that.

Most of their songs are instrumentals, but every so often the older woman will sing an Irish folk song or something in Gaelic. Then, another song started and Niamh sang . . . and I recognized it. She laid her violin down and the other young lady started playing solo while Niamh sang,

You know how long I've loved you

You know I love you still

Will I wait a lonely lifetime

If you want me to, I will.

And if I ever saw you

I didn't catch your name

But it never really matters

I will always feel the same.

Love you forever and forever

Love you with all my heart

Love you whenever we're together

Love you when we're apart.

And when at last I find you

Your song will fill the air

Sing it loud so I can hear you

Make it easy to be near you

Oh, the things you do

Endear you to me

Oh, you know I will.

I will.

Now I understand why she recognized those Beatles'
lyrics on the cliff that day.

I sat there on my stool totally mesmerized by the song and
her voice, not even noticing the old man patting me knee.
I could only dream she was singing to me. They took
another break after that song. I started to get up and make
my casual and disimpassioned walk by her, but the old
man wouldn't let go of my knee. For such an old man, he
had a firm hold of me, and was jabbering some jibberish I
never understood a single word of.

I gently pulled his hand from my leg, nodding and smiling appropriately, and started on my mission. Be cool, Mark. Don't do anything stupid, Mark. Act unconcerned and impassive, Mark. Just once, I wish I'd listen to myself!

As I got directly in front of her, five feet away, I couldn't help myself—I turned and looked. Those beautiful emerald eyes and that gorgeous face were staring back at me at the same time. Her lips parted, as if to say something, then suddenly someone grabbed my arm and jerked me sideways. Astonished by this, I turned and looked directly into Claire's face, just before she yelled, "I'm drunk!" Then she proceeded to kiss me in front of the entire pub— more importantly, five feet away from Niamh.

By the time I extricated myself from Claire's drunken embrace, I saw Niamh leaving the pub with the same guy I'd seen at her house that day. The other women in the group were still sitting there, gawking at me I presume. Or wondering why their violin player suddenly left the bar before they were finished.

"Claire! What are you doing?"

She rolled her eyes a little and again slurred, "I'm drunk!" Before I could say anything else, her eyes closed and she started slumping to the floor. I eased her down just as she vomited on my arms and shoes.

A couple of guys from the bar were happy to help me pick her up. They each took hold of a mini-skirted leg and left me to grab the puke covered upper half—nice guys! We found two other less drunk girls Claire had come with and laid her in their laps. Good luck!

As if by magic, as soon as Niamh finished singing one her favorite Beatles songs, which reminded her of that day on the cliff, he appeared right in front of her. And then, just as suddenly, some woman in a short skirt breaks the spell and kisses him right before her eyes. Even though her group had several other songs to perform, she motioned for her brother to follow her out. Without a word to anyone, she picked up her violin and her coat and left as quickly as she could.

When they were outside, her brother asked what was going on. "Why are we leaving? Niamh, what happened in there?"

"It was him. He was right in front of me."

"Who was right in front of you?"

"The man on the cliff that I kissed that day. He was somehow standing right in front of me."

Her brother didn't quite understand it all and said, "I thought you WANTED to see him again. Why did you leave?"

"Because he was kissing his girlfriend not five feet away from me. How can I be so daft? Let's go home."

By the time I extricated myself from the drunken Claire and cleaned a bit of the puke off of me, Niamh had gone. I went outside but only saw a car pulling away that looked like the car she was driving that day. I wandered back into the pub to check on Claire, who was blissfully passed out on a bench. One of her friends said, "I'm sorry about that. She seldom ever drinks and can't handle it very well."

I nodded and asked them, "Will you make sure she gets back home okay?"

"Sure. We're old school friends. We'll take care of her. I hope she didn't ruin your evening."

Well, ruined would be quite the understatement. So I just answered, "I've had a perfectly wonderful evening. But this wasn't it." It's okay to be angry, but it is never okay to be cruel. So I walked out to my car and drove home with the vision of Niamh, the emerald-eyed girl I can't forget, driving away with another man.

40

NIAMH ARRIVED AT HER HOUSE in tears. She couldn't explain to her brother why she was crying. She wasn't sure she understood it herself. How could she be this emotional over someone she only met for a few minutes one day high on a cliff? Sometimes, only the heart knows what the heart knows.

Her brother was still confused by what had happened and asked her to fully explain it to him. She said, "He was the man I drove up to the cliff that day and kissed, the American. I kept hoping I'd see him somewhere, sometime, someplace, and we would connect again. But I never saw him until tonight. I'd just finished singing and looked up and there he was. Our eyes met and I felt frozen in time. For just an instant, I thought everything in my life had culminated in that one moment. That my dreams had come true. Then, everything crashed when his girlfriend just had to kiss him right in front of me. RIGHT IN FRONT OF ME!"

Her crying became uncontrollable and all her brother could do was hold her until the agony and suffering became bearable again. Eventually, they both went to bed. Niamh was thankful her daughter was staying with her parents this weekend. She could barely take care of herself this night and wanted nothing more than to lie in bed by herself and curse the darkness and her own unrealistic dreams.

Her brother rose early and tried his best to prepare breakfast. The tea was drinkable. Fortunately for Niamh, she did not want anything to eat. They sat in silence before Niamh finally said, "I think you're right; I should move closer to Mom and Dad. Can you put me in touch with a realty agent in Clifden? There's no reason for me to stay here any longer."

I waited until church services ended before I left the apartment. I was not looking forward to facing Claire, but I needed to make sure she was okay and that the restaurant was open. When I walked in, she was at the register smiling and talking to an older couple about something—probably the weather. When they left, I walked over to her and before I could say anything, she looked at me and said, "My head's killing me! I don't know if I can make it all day."

Attempting to clarify if she was sick or only hungover, I asked her what was wrong. "I was out with some girlfriends last night and I think I ate something rotten. I feel terrible."

"Really? Where did you go?"

"To a pub in Burtonport. My girlfriends said there were lots of guys there, but I didn't see anyone worth noticing. It was a total waste of time."

"So you ate something there that made you sick?"

"Yes. I'm sure of it. I'll never go there again, that's for sure."

Apparently, she doesn't remember anything about last night. I certainly hope she doesn't remember kissing me! So I tell her, "Why don't you leave and go home, I'll check on the restaurant today and make sure things are okay. Go home and take care of yourself."

"Thanks, Mark, I really appreciate it. I'm so sorry, I don't know what I ate that's made me so sick."

I do—several glasses of Guinness, topped with shots of Irish whiskey!

I feel like a complete fool because of my actions last night. I intruded on Niamh and her boyfriend, then got involved with a drunken Amite. At least I can finally dismiss any notions of a green-eyed, dream girl. Oh well, I'm not where I want to be, but thank God I'm not where I used to be.

I was startled when the plump waitress called out my name. "Mark, phone call!"

I went to the phone and it was Mairead. "Mark, where have you been? I've been calling the pub all morning?" I had completely forgotten about Mairead and my flight to Dublin. "Can you get to Galway by 4:00? I have you a reservation."

"Yes. I'm sorry. We had a small problem at the restaurant. I'll leave now. Will you pick me up at the airport in Dublin?"

Yes. Hurry. I'll see you then. Hurry."

That last couple of phrases reminded me of General Custer's last message to his supply train just before he stumbled into a massacre: "Bring packs. Hurry. PS, bring packs!"

I throw some things in a small bag and drive to the Galway airport, relying on my NASCAR heritage to get me there on time. It was a relatively short and bumpy flight into the mayhem that is Dublin, all made worse by the impending doom I know I'm going to be facing. Trying to reason with Ailin regarding his relationship with Mairead is going to be a dreadful and probably impossible mission.

Mairead is indeed waiting for me with tears in her eyes and distress on her face. On the drive to her apartment, she tells me how Ailin has been following her and making veiled threats of what he will do if he can't win her back. She pleads with me to talk some sense into him and convince him to move back to Dungloe. It all sounds impossible to me.

I'm wondering how I'll contact Ailin to set up a meeting. Will Mairead call him? Does she want me to call him? These questions are answered when we pull up in front of her apartment and he is sitting on the steps waiting for us.

Much to my surprise, when I get out of the car Mairead steps on the gas and leaves. I turn to look at Ailin and he motions for me to come and sit with him on the steps. He doesn't seem surprised at all to see me. "Hello, Mark. Sorry you had to get involved in this."

At this point I know silence is my ally. He continues, "It's over and I know it. I tried my best, but it's just not what she wants. I'll be leaving now. You can tell her that, and also that I won't bother her again. If she ever wants to talk to me, she can call either you or the pub and they'll let me know."

"I'm sorry, Ailin. I truly am. I don't know what to say. Do you want me to travel back with you or would you rather go alone?"

"I'm not going back to Dungloe, Mark. You take care of things there. I know you'll do a good job with it."

"What do you mean? Where are you going?"

"That's not important. Just know that I'll be fine. I'm going somewhere to concentrate on my writing and try to forget the unforgettable. I'll keep in touch by email—very infrequently. You do what needs to be done. I know I can trust you."

I have no idea what to say or do. He gets up and shakes my hand, then turns and walks down the street and around the corner. And he's gone.

After about thirty minutes, Mairead drives by slowly. When she doesn't see Ailin sitting with me, she parks her car. I tell her what happened and she doesn't believe that he'll really leave. I try to convince her otherwise. I know a beaten man when I've seen one—Ailin is beaten.

41

MAIREAD WANTS ME to spend the night at her apartment, but I decline. There is no way I'm going to be there in case Ailin would happen to return. I tell her I'll check with her in the morning before I leave. Tonight, I want to visit the Temple Bar district of Dublin and see for myself if there are indeed some Irish lasses looking for American companionship.

The Temple Bar district is block after block of pubs, restaurants, and bars. On nearly every corner there are musicians playing and artists painting or drawing. This entire section of Dublin is vibrant and exciting—I understand why it draws young people from all over Ireland. After walking around and enjoying all the scenery, I finally enter one of the many pubs to have a bite to eat and something to drink. If some young ladies happen to be in there as well, that will indeed be a bonus.

It was a bonus. I'm pretty sure there are more women than men in this particular pub. A band is playing and people are dancing and drinking and generally having a grand time. I take a seat at the bar and have a sandwich and drink. Soon, a young lady sits next to me asking, "Is this seat taken?"

"No, ma'am, it's not."

"Are you from America?"

"Yes. But I'm living here now . . . not in Dublin, but here in Ireland."

She nods and crosses her legs, which are shapely and not well hidden by the short dress she's wearing. She continues to stare at me, but doesn't say anything, making me a little nervous. I finally ask if I can buy her a drink.

She says, "I'm not sure if I can trust an American, especially after I've had a few drinks. Can I trust you?"

I try to remember all the pick-up lines I learned from my days in North Carolina. I think of all the lies I could, and probably should, tell her. I take another look at her legs and then at her very pretty face and all I can imagine is a girl with emerald eyes and light brown hair, with a tinge of red.

I say, "No. You can't trust me. I wish you could, but you can't."

She only laughs at this and says, "Well, you're more honest than most Irishmen I know. Am I not your type?"

"You are the type of woman every man would want. But it seems as though I'm stuck with the thoughts of another young lady, and I can't seem to let it go."

By the end of my second Guinness, I had told her the entire sad saga of Niamh. I had even shown her the hair clip, which I can't seem to throw away. She called a girlfriend over and asked me to re-tell the story to her. When I finished the second version of my story, they were both crying. What a night. I come to Dublin to pick up a girl and end up making two girls cry. Niamh . . . what are you doing to me?

I check with Mairead in the morning and she's not seen or heard from Ailin. Instead of flying back to Galway, I opt to take the train so I can actually see the countryside as I travel. The train travels through many small towns and cities across the country. In nearly every one of them I see an old castle of some type. Some of the castles seem abandoned and run down, while others seem to have been restored and are quite magnificent.

We pass through large fields of heather, with glistening streams and mountains in the distance. The beauty of Ireland can take your breath away, whether you wish it to or not. I change trains in Galway and take another back to Dungloe, where I arrive in time for dinner at the restaurant. I walk in and find a table away from the crowd and see something absolutely stunning. Claire, the Amite turned cover girl, has reverted back to her tight-bunned Amish ways.

She sees me and walks over, but before I can ask why she's abandoned her short skirts and makeup, she says, "I couldn't take it anymore."

"Couldn't take what?"

"All the guys constantly eying me, groping me with their dirty little minds. And those shoes were killing me! I appreciate your advice, but that wasn't me. I have to be me, Mark. Unlike you, I can't live a lie." Then she says, "Your food will be right out."

I find the entire conversation extremely weird, especially the part about my food coming right out, since I haven't actually ordered anything yet. But if Ailin taught me anything, it is that silence is always the best answer.

I miss my daily cups of coffee with Ailin. And I miss my evening Guinness with him as well. It's obviously not the drinks though, it's the conversation and the advice that I long for. I just miss my friend. This is the excuse I give myself to go back to Burtonport and visit the pub where the girl band played and the bartender spoke with me. I don't go for morning coffee, but I do start going there each evening to "talk" with the bartender. Since my first time there, when I was asking him about the non-existent taxi, until the ill-fated night of the drunken Claire, he has been very friendly with me.

It also gives me an opportunity to visit the cliff. Yes, I still go up there. Now that I have a car to use, I just can't pass up the opportunity to drive up there and stare out into the ocean and dream. As I start up the winding road I almost hit a car coming down, which is very unusual because nobody ever goes up this road. At the top of the cliff, the wind is relentless. So I just sit in the car with all the electronic equipment and try to forget why I keep coming up here. I'm lousy at forgetting.

After several lonely remembrances, I wind my way back down to the pub and pull up a stool at the bar. I'm sure Jims wonders why someone who works at a bar in Dungloe keeps coming over to his bar in Burtonport. But he is adept at keeping his opinions and wonderings to himself. His name is actually James, but in his northern Irish accent, it sounds exactly like he's saying "Jims." So, to me, Jims it is.

He knows about the night the girls were playing. He witnessed most of it, including Claire passing out. He tells me the girls have not called him to come back and play— he hasn't heard from them. I tell him I hope I'm not bothering him, or others, by coming over here so much. He says, "If it matters to you, who cares if it matters to anyone else."

I say, "Jims, I probably made a mistake with Niamh (I've obviously told him her name and the complete story.)

He sort of smiles back and says, "You know what, Mark, some mistakes are too much fun to make only once."

So I drink a Guinness or two, tell him goodnight, clutch my pink hair clip with the little hearts all over it, and slowly drive back to Dungloe to my apartment over the pub.

42

NIAMH'S BROTHER found her a nice house on Sky Road in Clifden. Sky Road is a very small lane that winds up a medium-sized hill, then tops out with a view of the bay. Set out in the bay are dozens of little islands, some with a house or two, but mostly they're just used for grazing sheep. When the sun shines, the view is ridiculously unimaginable; when it's raining or cloudy, it's just simply beautiful. Niamh's new house is located on the high part of Sky Road with views up and down the coastline.

Niamh moved into the house soon after the debacle at the pub, when her dreams of an American were smashed by some floozy kissing him. She put her house in Annagry up for sale. As she was leaving her house for the last time, she also took a side trip up to the cliff in Burtonport, where something magical had happened to her, once upon a time . . . something she couldn't forget, no matter how many images of drunken floozies remained in her mind.

She sat up on the cliff in her car and stared out into the ocean. She thought of so many "what ifs" that her mind lost track of time. She brought herself back to reality and started the car back down the winding road. As she was near the bottom, she made the last turn before town and narrowly missed hitting another car coming up the road.

For an instant—for a millisecond—she glanced at the driver in the other car and almost convinced herself it could have been an American from the Northlands of Carolina.

My days are pretty routine now. All the businesses are running smoothly and everyone seems to have gotten over the shock of Ailin leaving. I drink my morning coffee quite alone—I miss Ruaraidh and Ailin. Today I decide to walk around town and enjoy the impending springtime weather, check on all the businesses, and finish up at the restaurant for breakfast. With spring, everyone's disposition changes. Well, almost everyone.

Without taking my order, Claire asks me out of the blue, "Were you having an affair with Mairead? Is that why she left?"

"Having an affair with Mairead? Are you daft girl? How could you possibly think that?"

"Well . . . you two used to sit around the pub and talk. Then you went to Galway one weekend with her and God only knows what you did there. Then, you ran off to Dublin to be with her. It's pretty obvious what's going on. You're in love with her!"

"Claire, things aren't what they seem to be and never were."

She smiles and replies, "Well that's not what everyone is saying about you."

I rise from the table and disgustedly throw my napkin down, saying, "If I worried what everyone was saying about me, I'd never leave my apartment. I'm exhausted by how stupid everyone is getting around here."

"Well, what are we supposed to think? You come into town and spend time with Mairead. Then she moves to Dublin and Ailin leaves us all. And to top it all off, you've been here nearly a year and haven't had one single, solitary date! Either you're gay or you've been having an affair with Mairead. Which is it?"

It's funny that sometimes when you feel like you're about to explode, some inner peace will come over you and reason with you. It may not always win, but sometimes, like now, you listen to this inner voice. As calmly as I possibly can, I say, "Claire, you're only as blind as you want to be." It was very satisfying walking out the door, seeing the look on her face, trying to understand what that meant.

I wind my way back over to Burtonport this afternoon and climb the hill up to the cliff of no return. My mother always told me, "Son, God always leads us where we need to be, not where we want to be." Well, Mom, I don't want to be here, but I need to be here. I know that I can't keep coming up here day after day. I'm fully aware that this is somewhat crazy . . . okay, it's a lot crazy. Soon, I'm going to throw this hair clip away and stop this foolish trip up the cliff every day . . . soon. I look at myself in the rearview mirror and feel as though I took a fall, missed the ground, and just kept on falling.

After a suitable period of time for recovery, I go to the pub and see that my new friend Jims has a pint waiting on me. I'm getting way too predictable. He says, "I have some news for you. The girls are coming back to play Saturday." Instantly, my entire disposition brightens. Jims says, "They'll be here about half nine Saturday night, then winks at me and says, "Don't be late."

Waiting for Saturday night is difficult. I avoid the restaurant and eat all my meals in the pub to avoid any Amish confrontations. Thursday evening, Turlough comes in the pub, looks at me and says, "We've got to talk."

We go back to the corner table Ailin and I used to sit at and wait for the waitress to leave before he explains, "We've got to do something. The boys are getting itchy. If you don't calm them down and come up with something soon, I think they'll do something crazy on their own."

"Okay, okay . . . set up a meeting and we'll get together and come up with something. But first, tell them they do NOTHING without all of us agreeing on it. Call me back when you talk to them and let me know when we can meet. Oh, Turlough, we can meet anytime except Saturday night. Let me know."

I meet with the boys and Turlough Friday night. They have several ideas, none of which seem reasonable to me, but I know we'd better find some project just to keep them from doing something crazy. We finally decide on another computer scam. It's fairly ingenious and relatively safe. Our computer whiz is going to hack into the Belfast Department of Transportation and send out messages early Monday morning saying that the main bridge into the city is closed. All electronic signs on the highway will start flashing, "Bridge Closed." There will be traffic jams of monumental proportions.

We all agree and they seem very happy to create chaos for the Brits. Turlough and I have no part in the actual implementing of this project; we only agree and give our approval. They do ask if I'll notify Ailin to keep him abreast of what we're doing. I agree, even though I have no idea how to contact Ailin. But they don't need to know that—just yet.

Time slowed so badly on Saturday that I started to call Stephen Hawking to see if he could help. The morning drug by, the afternoon crawled and I'm certain my clock was stuck this evening. The anticipation of seeing the girl band and Niamh again was excruciating for me. I arrive at the pub fully two hours before they are to play and tell myself to "sip" only. I want to be in full control of my senses when I have the chance to talk with Niamh and explain what happened with Claire kissing me.

Finally, around 9:20 things start happening. A space is cleared and people are milling around waiting for the music. I see the girls come from the back—all except Niamh. Instead, there is a younger, new girl carrying a violin case. She does not have green eyes. She does not have light brown hair with a tinge of red. She does not possess that gorgeous face and she is definitely not my Niamh.

I take a seat at the bar and wait, hoping against hope, that maybe Niamh will arrive late. She does not. Jims ambles over to me with a pint that I haven't ordered and says, "Here, you look like you might need this." I didn't say it, but I thought to myself, "Jims, I need way more than this." I don't even have the desire to taste the glass of black brew. After a couple of songs from the band, I slip out the door and get in my car. Inexplicably, almost as if benumbed or paralyzed, I drive up to the cliff.

By some minor weather miracle, the wind is not blowing very hard. Even though it's dark, the moon does illuminate the white spray of the waves crashing on the shore. I get out and sit down, leaning against the car the same way I did that day with Niamh, over 300 years ago. "Mark," I tell myself, "you've got to stop this. You've got to forget this girl and this crazy infatuation you have. She's gone and you have to move on. Throw that hair clip away—OVER THE CLIFF. Get on with your life, boy."

For the first time in months, what I tell myself actually makes sense. Even though it's dark, I can somehow see the light now. I have a new perspective and I feel better—not great but better. I sit a little longer and take several deep breaths, then stand up and as hard as I can, I throw a rock over the cliff. That being done, I get back in my car and drive the curvy road down the cliff, clutching my pink hair clip, with little hearts on it, as hard as I can.

43

"THE BOYS" little prank turned into a major disaster for the British government. On Monday morning, no one knew why all the road signs starting flashing "Bridge Closed." They were definitely not prepared for the major traffic jams that ensued. It was the top news story on all the networks and papers. Ailin would be proud of us, if he only knew it WAS us.

Then, Monday evening as I was preparing to drive over to Burtonport, I received an email from Ailin. All it says is that he's fine, not to worry about him, and to reassure Mairead he'll never bother her again. He also wants me to tell her he'll take care of the house in Dungloe and handle all the expenses. I'm sure he's hanging on to the house in the faint hope of a future reconciliation. He has his dreams, and I have mine.

An idea suddenly pops in my head—which lately has been pretty dangerous. I forward the email from Ailin to my IRA friend who is fantastic with computers. As I forward it, I delete Ailin's name and any reference of him or Mairead. I then add some non-descript dribble that he won't be interested in. It's not the context of the message that's important, I want him to trace this message and tell me where it originated from.

I tell him an old girlfriend sent it to me and I'm trying to figure out where she is. Anything that references a "girl" will be sure to garner his attention. I send this to him before I set out for my daily cliff trip to Burtonport, hoping he'll get back to me in a day or two. But before I can even close my computer, I have a return message from him. The message originated in London, from the Covent Garden area in the city center. That's as close as he can narrow it down without further information.

London? What on God's green earth is Ailin doing in London? He hates the Brits and hates anything to do with the Brits. This can't be good; however, it'll probably be worse for the English than it will be for Ailin.

As I'm making the drive over to Burtonport today, I change my mind and decide to ride out to Niamh's house in Annagry, instead of the cliff. I promise myself I won't stop. I tell myself I'm not a stalker. Then I wonder why I keep lying to myself. I will slow down, however, as I approach her house in the hopes I might see her outside. Or, maybe if she's checking her mail, or picking up her paper, I could assist her and provide a valuable service. I'm good that way. As I approach her house it has the unmistakable appearance of being vacant: no curtains in the windows, no lights on inside, no wreath on the door, and the grass needs to be cut.

Can things get any worse? I pull over to the side of the road, mainly because I'm incapable of driving at the moment. Let me review my life in a nutshell. My business nearly fails. My wife leaves me. Her lawyer threatens me. My new friend Ruaraidh dies. My other new friend moves to London. My lady friend, Mairead, moves to Dublin. The Amite thinks I might be gay. The one girl in the whole universe that I can't forget has moved away—and I don't know where. It ain't easy being me.

I can't bear to drive up to the cliff today or visit the pub in Burtonport. Sadly, I return to Dungloe and go to my apartment above the pub to re-think my life and my options.

I take a short sabbatical from the cliff and don't go over on Tuesday. I do visit Jims, however, and he apologizes for my disappointment with the band Saturday night. He says he didn't know about the new violin player and does not know what happened to the old girl—my girl. I lie and tell him it's okay. I think he can see the despair and disappointment on my face, so he says, "I've got a joke for you. How many Germans does it take to screw in a light bulb? One! They're very efficient and not very funny."

As he finishes telling me the joke, a rather short, undistinguished guy in his late twenties comes up to the bar and says, "Pa, can you loan me twenty Euros?" Without uttering a single word, Jims takes a 20 Euro note from his pocket and hands it to him. His son says, "Thanks, Pa. You're the greatest." He leaves the pub with a plain-looking young lady with purple frosting in her hair.

When they leave, I look at Jims and tell him, "You're a great dad, Jims."

He gives me a tight little grin and replies, "I'm a GOOD dad because I still let him live at home for free. If I had the nerve to kick him out and make him fend for himself, I'd be a GREAT dad." I ask Jims about his son and what he does for a living. Jims sighs, then shakes his head and says, "All his life, I always wanted him to be somebody. Now I see that I should have been more specific." And once again, silence is my best response. Thank you, Ailin.

Niamh loves her new house; she just hates her life. She misses the girls she played music with. She misses her part-time job. She misses all the teachers at her daughter's school. Most of all, she misses the opportunity she may have had to accidentally bump into an American roaming around the outskirts of Annagry. It's hard for her to explain to her parents and her brother, and, indeed, to herself how an American with longish-hair and a scraggly goatee makes her feel. She tells herself, "Niamh, you've got to stop watering dead plants." But as she hears this in her mind, her other voice tells her, "Girl, if you don't imagine, nothing ever happens at all."

So, she takes her daughter to school, comes home, cooks, and does laundry. Then she sits by the window with a cup of tea and gazes out Sky Road at one of the most amazing scenes God ever created . . . and wishes she was sitting on a wind-blasted cliff outside of Burtonport with a long-haired man from the Northlands of Carolina.

44

I HAVE STAYED AWAY from the restaurant all week, but it's been hard. Not that I'm missing Claire, but because I am missing my full Irish breakfast of ham, bacon, sausage, baked beans, eggs, and fried tomato (not the tomato). I am happy there are no scales in the pub or my apartment. This way I am positive I have gained no weight. I feel pretty confident a full Irish breakfast and a couple of nutritious Guinnesses at the end of the day are a well-balanced addition to my life. And as my friend Ruaraidh used to say, "It's all fun and games till your jeans don't fit anymore." Ah, Ruaraidh. How I miss you.

It's a rainy, cool Saturday and I choose to stay inside. Even though the calendar may say "summer," the weather still says "Ireland." I forego my daily cliff trip and decide to hang around the pub tonight and listen to some music. Rumor has it that the boy musical genius, Conloath, is going to play and I don't want to miss that.

I roam around the pub and talk with a few friends waiting for the music to start. I'd like to talk with our new bartender, but he's the strong, silent type. No matter how many times I've tried to initiate a conversation with him, it all becomes fruitless by his silence. Otherwise, he does a great job. He's just not the conversationalist Ruaraidh was. The only time we had a meaningful discussion was when I was trying to get him to open up a bit with the customers. I told him some of the regulars might think he was a bit of a snob by not talking to them. He raised his chin a little and said, "A lion never loses sleep over the opinions of sheep."

Conloath did play again tonight and mesmerized the crowd with his brilliance. I also heard that his parents are entertaining thoughts of moving to either Dublin or London to further their son's musical education and opportunities. I hope for us, it's Dublin. Just as Conloath finishes his last hypnotizing solo and runs into his parent's arms, I see Claire enter the pub.

She seldom visits our bar, so I'm a little surprised to see her tonight, even more so when I notice she's with a girlfriend. Or, at least it's a girl and I assume they're friends. There could not be two more diverse looking young ladies in all of Ireland. Claire is of course back to her Amish ways, dressed in the usual long, baggy dress, with her hair in an unusually tight bun. Her friend, however, looks as though she's on her way to a party at the Playboy mansion in Hollywood: short dress; very high heels, coiffed, platinum blonde hair; and enough makeup to soft-putty the gaping hole in our bar.

Everyone in the pub stares as the two polar opposites walk my way. Claire speaks first, saying, "Hello, Mark, I want to introduce you to my friend, Ashleen. I've told her all about you."

"Well, that's interesting. Very nice to meet you, Ashleen. Have you two been friends long?"

Ashleen bats her eyes several times before answering, "Oh, yes, I've known Mary quite a while."

I clarify, "You mean Claire?"

She quickly looks Claire's way and replies, "Yes, I'm sorry. Claire . . . of course."

At this point in this ever-increasingly weird conversation, Claire interrupts and says, "Oh, I just remembered, I have to go take my mum some medicine. Will you entertain Ashleen till I get back?"

And without giving me a chance to answer that insane question, she turns and walks her Amish self out of the pub. Ashleen looks at me. I look at her. And we both wonder, "What's next?" I found the answer to that very quickly.

Ashleen asks, "Would you like to buy me a drink?"

I motion for my silent bartender to come over. When he arrives, he says, "Hey, Ashleen. Have you recovered yet?"

As she non-answers him, I'm thinking, "Recovered from what? And how does he know Ashleen?"

I say, "Bring us two pints, please."

But Ashleen corrects me, saying, "I'll have a shot of Bushmill's—and, make it a double."

If I even smell Bushmill's, it almost makes me pass out. Who is this girl? As the bartender leaves to get our drinks, I say, "Excuse me, I'll be right back."

I follow him down the bar and say to him, "Do you know her? What's she recovering from?"

He looks back as he's pouring the whiskey, winks at me, and says, "You'll find out."

The Amite does not return. Ashleen drinks four double shots of Bushmill's and is still conscious. I don't know how. She finally slurs something that sounds like, "Can't we go up to your place for a bit?"

"We'd better not, Ashleen. I think I'd better get you home."

"No . . . I want to go up to your place Mark. I told Mary I'd show you a good time."

I knew the Amite was behind this! Knowing that most Irish girls are Catholics and trying to play off her Catholic upbringing, I say to her, "That's probably not a good idea, Ashleen. Isn't premarital sex one of the worst sins you can commit?"

She leans in close to me and whispers, "It's not premarital sex if you have no intention of getting married."

This is one of those occasions where it's good to be the boss. I motion for the bartender to come over and say to him, "You know her. You take her home. Now! I'll manage the bar till you get back." He starts to say something and I look fiercely in his eyes and order, "NOW!"

I am so mad at Claire I can't think straight. Even when I go to bed I can't stop thinking about this entire episode. It didn't help any either that it took my bartender nearly two hours to take her home, on what should have been a ten minute trip.

I wait till after church Sunday, then go to the restaurant to face the Amite from Hades. When I walk in and don't see her anywhere, I remembered she's off today. I ask one of the girls to get her on the phone for me. She makes the call and hands me the phone. "Claire, I'm at the restaurant. I need to talk to you."

"I'm off today. Come by tomorrow."

"No," I say rather firmly, "I need to talk to you now."

"Well go ahead and talk then. I guess since you're the boss, I have no choice in the matter."

Sometimes she makes me so mad I could chew rocks. But I don't want to wait another day so I tell her, "I don't appreciate what you did last night. It was demeaning to me and to your friend."

"She's not my friend. I was doing you a favor."

"Favor? By pushing some floozy on me at the pub?"

Silence for a few seconds, then she says, "Well did you have a good time?"

"No! I had a terrible time."

"Why? Was she not as good as she says she is?"

"I have no idea whether she's good or not. I made the bartender take her home."

"Well, at least somebody had a good time. That just proves my point."

"Proves what?"

Silence. More silence. Finally, I ask again, "Proves what, Claire?"

"You know." And the phone goes dead. I call back and it's busy.

I'm waiting for her early Monday morning at the restaurant. I want to settle this once and for all. She walks up and I say, "What makes you think I need you to get me a girl?"

She looks at me from my shoes to the top of my head, and says, "I'm not sure it's a GIRL you need."

"Claire, I'll tell you this again and it better never come up again. I'm not gay."

"Okay, if you say so. But if you're not gay, then why did you turn down a sure thing last night?"

"Because maybe some of us have higher standards than others. And maybe I'm just like you."

She seems taken back by this comment of mine, "What do you mean, just like me?"

"Apparently sex is not the top priority in the lives of either of us."

She then smiles for the first time in months and says, "Speak for yourself." She turns abruptly and enters the restaurant, leaving me somehow to comprehend that last statement of hers.

45

I'M APPROACHING MY ONE YEAR anniversary here in Dungloe. I never thought it would feel so much like home, but it does. Turlough and the boys came up with another computer scheme to make life miserable for the Brits in Northern Ireland. I quickly approved it, mainly because it left me completely out of actually doing anything. I don't mind being part of the IRA as long as I don't get in trouble for it. When Ailin was in charge, I'd probably have done anything to help him. But now that they rely on me, I'm a little hesitant to take on any controversial missions. The computer schemes and malfunctions work out perfectly for us all.

I received another short email from Ailin regarding some financial instructions for payments of bills. He gave no other personal information or asked any questions. I hope he's okay. Mairead called me last night to ask about him, but mainly just to talk. She seems happy and is very busy. She's started working full-time at the university again and is busy with concerts, recitals, and art shows. I know that at some point she'll get involved with a man in Dublin. She's too beautiful for men to ignore. Just as I'm sure Niamh is either involved with the same guy I've seen her with twice now, or with someone new. She, also, is too beautiful for men to ignore.

Last week I went to the pub in Burtonport every night, but only visited the cliff three times—I'm getting better. The last time I drove up there I saw a car similar to Niamh's parked near the edge, which temporarily excited me, but it was just two teenagers necking. When I surprised them, they were both in various stages of undress. So I went over to an old yew tree, which grew near the edge, and sat looking out into the ocean. I was in such a state of contemplation that I thought I could have written an entire book on that yew tree. Not all yew trees, just that particular one. What it had experienced over the years— the strong winds, the rain, the storms, the snow, and the one day that it actually saw a man from the Northlands of Carolina kiss a girl from Tir-na-nOg. What a story that yew tree could tell if only I knew how to coax the story out of its silence and write it.

I enjoy visiting Jims, my new friend. He's fun to talk with and I love listening to his stories of old Ireland. Yesterday, Jims told me he had some "bad news." The girl band called to book another night with him and he asked the older woman what happened to the pretty fiddle player. She told him she wasn't exactly sure; she only told them that she was moving near her family—that was all. He thought I'd like to know. I didn't really. I'd rather keep holding on to my far-fetched dream.

Last week Jims vowed to set me up with a true "Irish princess." I was fairly excited by this impending blind date, until I met her for drinks the following night. She may have been an "Irish princess" back in Jims' youth— not any longer. I'm sure he meant well. But for the time being, I'll just continue holding onto my hair clip and dreaming thoughts of an emerald-eyed princess.

Several days, Niamh had to fight the urge to drive back to Burtonport and visit the cliff. She almost convinced herself that she should go back to her unsold house in Annagry to check on it. And since Burtonport was on the way, what harm would it do to drive up to that windy wasteland for a visit? Unfortunately, or fortunately as the case may be, picking her daughter up from school prevented any illusional and impractical day trips to that wilderness, wasteland of a cliff.

Every week she was turning down more requests for dates than the youngest, or oldest, or most forgettable Kardashian would get. Her brother could not understand what was happening with his sister. Her mother was concerned her only daughter was going to end up a spinster and not provide her with any more grandchildren. Her father only said, "Niamh, you cannot make everybody happy. You're not chocolate."

Finally, just to stop all the nagging, she accepted a date from a nice local man in Clifden. He was a car dealer and drove a new Toyota, which impressed most of the townspeople. His name was Quinlan and he was quite handsome. He took Niamh to the best restaurant in

Clifden and ordered a very expensive wine to impress her. She actually wanted a Guinness but settled for the over-priced, bland tasting red wine instead. After dinner, they went to a local pub and listened to music, while between songs Quinlan told her all about the car business. Which was thoroughly more than she ever wanted to know about the car business.

When they returned to Niamh's house after the date, Quinlan tried to kiss her goodnight. Niamh quickly turned away and he ended up kissing the area between her ear and chin instead. She made the excuse, or lie as it turned out, that her daughter was calling for her inside and she had to attend to her. Her daughter was, in fact, at her parent's house several miles away. Quinlan didn't mind. Nearly everyone in town had seen him out with a beautiful woman and this was certain to enhance his reputation with his friends and with any prospective car buyers.

At the urging of her mother, Niamh went out with Quinlan once more. But at the end of that date, when Quinlan tried to invite himself inside her house, Niamh had to tell him she simply wasn't interested in furthering this relationship. He was nice. He was handsome. He, apparently had his own money and wasn't interested in her insurance settlement. But . . . he wasn't an American with longish hair and a scraggly goatee who kissed her once, high on a cliff, better than anyone had ever kissed before.

Niamh made herself a cup of tea and stared out the window into the night, at the white spray of the waves as they crashed along the dozens of little islands out in the bay along Sky Road. Niamh has a beautiful daughter, whom she loves with all her heart. She has a fantastic house with incredible views and has all the money she will ever need. But, nothing is worth it if you aren't happy.

She knows she'll eventually meet someone nice, someone who will make her happy, someone whose kiss will make her dream. She knows that will happen. But not until she forgets how the American made her feel, and how he made her dream. She'll forget about him one day. She's almost certain of it.

I have a quiet truce now with the Amish witch. She doesn't speak to me and it makes us both happy. This morning, as I'm finishing my full Irish breakfast, I start reading a paper someone has left behind. There's a small article on the fourth page that catches my attention. It appears as though someone in London printed about 10,000 posters with the Queen's picture and a caption that read, "Free Ireland!" These posters were distributed around central London one night by unknown people. No one has taken credit for the prank and the police are still investigating. I am quite certain that Ailin is mightily enjoying his morning cup of tea today.

I'm also certain that something is going on with my new silent bartender and the Amite. Several times when he's been off, I've noticed that Claire is not at the restaurant. Coincidence? I hope not. They deserve each other—one can't shut up and the other one can't talk. They're a perfect couple.

Unfortunately for my subconscious, inner-self, I revert back to my daily habit of visiting the cliff this week; however, I compromise by only visiting the pub in Burtonport three or four times instead of every day. It's probably not a good sign when each time you walk into a bar, the bartender already has a pint of Guinness waiting on you. That's why I visit the cliff more often—it asks no questions and requires no explanations. It's just there—with the wind blowing, wondering why a crazy American clutching a pink hair clip with little hearts won't throw it over the side into the ocean.

Summer in Ireland is the best! Warm days and cool nights make it fantastic. I drive over to the coast, near where Mairead lived, and stop along the road every half mile or so to enjoy the views. Islands dot the shoreline and mountains can be seen inland; it's truly a magical place. It won't be long until the tourist industry discovers us up here all by ourselves. Until then, we're left to wander and wonder at all the sights God has bestowed on this land.

I usually take a small cooler with something to drink and a couple of sandwiches with me as I follow the meandering coastline. I have no agenda; in fact, sometimes I get myself quite lost, but there's always the GPS to get me home. I was driving around the countryside one day, having no idea where I actually was, and came upon a small church with an ancient round tower next to it. I stopped to investigate and found the small cemetery at the church had the grave of William Butler Yeats, one of Ireland's most famous literary figures. I walked to the gravesite, then toured the church, and finally went to the round tower, which was over 1100 years old.

Ireland is like that. Castles are dotted all over the land, ranging from those over a thousand years old to the relatively newer ones only a couple of hundred years old. All of them fascinating. It was getting a bit late so I said adieu to W.B. Yeats, checked the direction on my GPS, and took off for home. After driving for an hour and a half, I once again came upon a round tower, with a small church that had the grave of W.B. Yeats. What in the world have I done?

After several more wrong turns, I think I'm on the correct road back to Dungloe. It's much easier taking the train— trust me. I have to stop in a small town called Glenties to visit the restroom and get more gas for the car. As I'm paying for the gas and a Coke, I ask the middle-aged guy at the counter exactly how far Dungloe is from here.

He says, "Where?"

Thinking he either didn't understand my North Carolina accent, or else didn't hear me, I repeat, "Dungloe."

He looks at me quizzically for a moment and replies, "Is it around here?"

"Yes. It couldn't be far. Have you lived here long?"

He says, "Not really. I moved here as a boy."

If he moved here as a boy, and he's now around 40-45 years old, that means he's been living here for over three decades and has never heard of a neighboring town only ten miles away. And it doesn't surprise me. I pay him and wish him a grand and happy day, while thinking, "Only in Ireland."

46

NIAMH HAD JUST ARRIVED back home from dropping her daughter off at school when the phone rang. It was the realty company in Annagry notifying her that someone wanted to buy her house. Apparently, a retired geography professor from Appalachian State University in America wanted a summer home away from the maddening crowds in the south and west of Ireland. He was interested in something he and his wife could move into quickly and liked the price of Niamh's house. If she accepted the offer, the agent wanted to know when she could come to his office in Annagry and sign the papers.

To actually sell her house would absolutely close the door on any dream she still imagined of her illusory American. It took her three days to finally accept the offer. Her daughter and brother could not understand why such an apparently happy occasion caused her to cry so much. She told the agent she would come over and sign the papers on Friday. Her mother would keep her daughter after school so Niamh wouldn't have to rush back.

Even though the wind still blows pretty hard, the view from the cliff is even better during summer. The sun takes longer to actually change from bright yellow to rosy amber hues as it dips into the ocean. Some days I don't even hold the hair clip in my hand as I sit here. I leave it in my pocket, trying to wean myself off this drug called Niamh that I've become addicted to.

We have a big outdoor summer party planned at the pub on Saturday. It should be one of the biggest events of the season in Dungloe, so I'll only have one more day, Friday, to visit Jims and my lonely cliff before the party. I only wish Ruaraidh was here to experience the event we're planning. He would definitely be in his element. Saturday will take everyone at the pub working to make sure it runs smoothly. Then, it will probably take us all day Sunday (after church) to clean everything up. I'm looking forward to relaxing Friday afternoon with Jims and watching the sun set from my cliff before all the excitement of Saturday.

Just as I'm about to leave for Burtonport Friday afternoon, my silent bartender actually speaks to me. I'm so surprised at this rare occurrence that I don't notice Claire coming in the front door. Before I can ask any questions, Claire looks at me and says, "We're eloping! We need to be off next week."

I'm not entirely sure who she's eloping with. I hope she's not referring to me! Then I get it. My silent bartender and the Amite have indeed been seeing each other. He says, "I need to take off next week. We're going to Portugal." As he's telling me this, Claire puts her arms around him and kisses him.

Just because it's Claire—and I owe her—I ask my silent friend, "Who are you going with?"

My mind is blank as all I hear is "Blah, blah, blah, blah, blah." When Claire finally shuts up and I can quit smiling, I tell them, "Great! I'm happy for you both. But you are going to wait until after the weekend aren't you?" All is well—they're not leaving until Monday afternoon.

But Claire can't let me win. She says, "If this whole party thing wrecks our plans, I'm blaming you, Mark!"

I'm startled and reply, "Blaming me? Why is it my fault?"

And then with that devilish grin of hers, she snorts, "I didn't say it was your fault. I said I was blaming you!" And with that being said, she grabs the silent man's arm and drags him back into my office.

Well, some days you just have to create your own sunshine. I wait for my bartender to finish whatever he and the Amite are doing in my office so I can leave for Burtonport. I do not disturb them and I definitely don't want to know what they're up to.

When I'm sure my bartender is focused enough to function on his own, I leave for Burtonport. Today, I think I'll do double duty—I'll ride by the cliff and visit

Jims at the pub. Half way over to Burtonport I realize I've left the hair clip in my other pants. No choice, I have to turn around and go back—no choice. I drive back and run upstairs, thinking, "What are you doing, Mark? This is crazy." Safely inside my pocket now, the pink hair clip and I start back to the cliff. As usual, there's no one up here when I arrive and, for some odd meteorological reason, there's very little wind today. So instead of sitting in my car, out of the wind, I walk near the edge of the cliff and sit on a large rock to contemplate my strange obsession with this crazy hair clip.

I should've stayed in the car. As soon as I sit on the rock all sorts of weird thoughts start running through my mind. Maybe it's the fresh air or the wind currents shooting up the side of the cliff—I don't know. But I seem to have come to a point of clarity I haven't had in months. The point of clarity being, this is crazy! Holding on to this hair clip is crazy. Thinking Niamh is somehow going to magically appear back in my life is also crazy. Give it up, Mark!

I sit and hold the hair clip in my hands and dream of that day, on this very spot, where my life changed. Let it go, Mark! I can't keep living in the past. I realize that now. I can't keep carrying around this hair clip which reminds me of a dream I'll never realize. I must accept Niamh is gone. She's gone, Mark. Gone.

I take one long, lasting look at it, then lay the pink hair clip, with little hearts all over it, on the rock. I don't have the courage to throw it over the side, like I should.

Hopefully, when the wind inevitably picks up again, a strong gust will take it over the horizon to the land of Tir-na-nOg and reunite it with the girl with emerald eyes and light brown hair.

Having left the hair clip on the rock, I get back in my car and drive back down the curvy road to the pub before I lose my courage. Jims greets me, but he can tell my mind is elsewhere. He brings me a Guinness, nods, and smiles while walking away. I'll finish this pint and drive back home. I'll come back and visit Jims—maybe not as often as before, but I know I will. However, I won't come back to the cliff. I'll choose to always remember it for the day I kissed the girl from Tir-na-nOg

Friday afternoon Niamh signs all the appropriate documents for the sale of her house. After all the paperwork is done, she rides out to her now ex-house and parks in the driveway and cries. An important part of her life is now gone—the only house her daughter has ever known and the house where she grieved when her husband died is gone. Now, she must go to another place and put it behind her as well. She backs out of the driveway and starts driving for a certain high cliff just outside of Burtonport.

She drives up the curvy road and is surprised to find the wind very calm this afternoon. She parks her car and gets out to breathe it all in. Breathing deeply, she remembers this very spot where she once kissed an American from the Northlands of Carolina, a kiss unlike any other in her life and, she's almost certain, one that won't be equaled anytime soon. She tries to compose herself while thinking, "No more. I won't come back here again." But today, she can remember. Today, she can dream . . . and it's okay.

After a few moments, she remembers she must get back to Clifden and pick up her daughter. There's no time to loiter and reminisce over unrealistic dreams. She stares out over the edge one last time and something out of place catches her eye. Something pink is lying on a rock over near the cliff side. She walks over to the rock and nearly collapses. She's having a hard time breathing and an even harder time understanding. A pink hair clip with little hearts all over it is sitting on the rock. The same type hair clip that is holding her hair back now. The same hair clip that she, once upon a time, used to clip the hair back on an American with a scraggly goatee.

How? Why? Where did this come from? She turns and looks in all directions—nothing. Nothing to see and no explanation for what she has seen. She puts the pink hair clip in her pocket and tries to breathe normally. She gets back in her car and as soon as her hands stop trembling, she starts the engine and slowly winds her way back down the curvy road.

So, the man from the Northlands of Carolina and girl from Tir-na-nOg will continue their quest for enchantment and magic and love for the next three hundred years, which to them will only seem like three weeks.

Thanks, Larry.

About Gary Hope

The author lives a thoroughly enjoyable and blessed life with his beautiful wife, a fantastic family, and the best friends known to man. If you wish to read his other works of fiction, they are:

"It's Too Late To Die Young Now"

And

"Abbey"

www.ingramcontent.com/pod-product-compliance
Lightning Source LLC
Chambersburg PA
CBHW071106250626
47159CB00002B/616